MISTRESS OF WAR
BOOK 1

Other books by R. A. Steffan

The Complete Horse Mistress Collection
The Complete Lion Mistress Collection
The Complete Dragon Mistress Collection
The Complete Master of Hounds Collection

Circle of Blood: Books 1-3
Circle of Blood: Books 4-6
(with Jaelynn Woolf)

The Last Vampire: Books 1-3
The Last Vampire: Books 4-6
(with Jaelynn Woolf)

Vampire Bound: Complete Series, Books 1-4
Forsaken Fae: The Complete Series, Books 1-3
The Sixth Demon: Complete Series, Books 1-4

Antidote: Love and War, Book 1
Antigen: Love and War, Book 2
Antibody: Love and War, Book 3
Anthelion: Love and War, Book 4
Antagonist: Love and War, Book 5

Diamond Bar Apha Ranch
Diamond Bar Alpha 2: Angel & Vic
(with Jaelynn Woolf)

MISTRESS OF WAR
BOOK 1

R. A. STEFFAN

Mistress of War: Book 1: Book 1

Copyright 2024 by R. A. Steffan

ISBN: 978-1-955073-84-4 (paperback)

For information, contact the author at
http://www.rasteffan.com/contact/

Cover by Ember

First Edition: October 2024

Author's Note

This book contains descriptions of graphic sex and violence. It is intended for a mature audience.

TABLE OF CONTENTS

ONE

When an assassin pulled a dagger during the middle of the emperor's summer soirée, it was almost a relief.

Now, to be fair, I had nothing against parties in general. I also had nothing against dancing at parties. I wasn't even totally averse to drunken strangers grabbing my arse while I was dancing at parties.

I did, however, draw the line when those drunken strangers were old enough to be my grandfather—and there had been a fair amount of that kind of thing this evening. Nevertheless, when I saw the dagger glint in the hand of an oily little weasel of a man making his way toward Emperor Kaeto's retinue, I did what any self-respecting hired dancing girl would do.

I screamed *"Assassin!"* at the top of my lungs. Then I grabbed the nearest burning oil lamp and hurled it at the man's head.

The results were quite satisfying if you were into that kind of thing... which I strenuously maintain that I wasn't. The bronze lamp impacted my target's shoulder, dislodging its metal lid and splattering him with flammable oil. In a flash of luck—good or bad, depending on your point of view—the lamp's still-burning wick slapped against the oil-soaked sleeve of his ornate embroidered robes. Flames whooshed, enveloping his left arm and spreading rapidly outward from there.

The man shrieked, his dagger clattering to the marble floor as he whirled this way and that, slapping at his clothing and generally making the situation much worse than if he'd simply dropped to the floor and rolled around a bit to smother the burning cloth. Within seconds, several of the guards who'd been unobtrusively stationed around the grand space converged on him. One of them pulled a tapestry down from the nearest wall and bore the man to the ground beneath it, using the heavy woven cloth to stifle the flames.

I hoped the tapestry hadn't been valuable.

A familiar presence rumbled to life at the back of my mind, because of *course* I needed an uninvited second voice inside my head right now.

Fire good. Tapestries stupid, it said.

Shut up, I thought. *This isn't really the time.*

I received the brief impression of an amused eye roll before the presence quieted, and I was once more able to turn my full attention outward.

It was a testament to how desperate the partygoers were to make a good impression on their emperor that most of them hadn't immediately stampeded for the exits. Either that, or it was a testament to how common assassination attempts had become in the Alyrion Empire of late. For all I knew, watching a foiled assassin be set on fire during a party like this one was considered high entertainment—like the festive solstice bonfires back in my grandparents' village.

Whatever the case, most of the guests and entertainers had only retreated to the edges of the room. Once it became apparent that the fire was under control and wouldn't spread, the buzz of conversation swelled as they pressed forward to ogle the aftermath.

In the general scramble to get out of the way, I'd been left standing alone in the center of the atrium, abandoned by my fellow dancers as well as the musicians who'd been playing for us.

In my experience, when you were the hired entertainment, being singled out by powerful people wasn't usually a good thing. Under the circumstances, though, I felt like my odds were decent. A moment later, a sandy-haired guard who'd smoothly stepped in front of Emperor Kaeto during the confusion lifted his sword to point at me.

"You. Young woman. Approach us." Even if I hadn't already learned his name from palace gossip, the guard's tone of understated command would have marked him as a high-ranking tribuni.

Aelio, the others had named him. *The emperor's personal guard. A fair man, but don't cross him.*

Behind him, Kaeto's gray gaze was cool and assessing as it swept over me from head to foot, taking in my skimpy dancer's garb with a raised eyebrow. I jerked my attention downward to my own feet before I could accidentally offend him.

According to general opinion, the new emperor was better in some ways than his warmongering father had been... and worse in others. He was also, by all accounts, quite a bit prettier to look at. I could see the appeal of those sharp, hawklike features, topped by waves of thick, raven hair tucked beneath his gold crown. That didn't mean staring at him openly was in any way a smart idea.

I kept my gaze fixed on my bare toes as I walked forward, dropping into a low bow a few paces away from the tribuni's polished leather boots.

"Your Imperial Majesty," I murmured to the floor.

"Rise, girl." Kaeto's voice was as sharp as his features. "You did a service to your emperor tonight. Go with my guard. I would have him speak with you."

I glanced up, rising to my feet with what I sincerely hoped was a dancer's grace. At Aelio's crooked finger, two more guards approached to flank the emperor — replacing him as he sheathed his sword and gestured me to precede him toward one of the side exits.

Heart thudding, I made my way through the soaring archway. Aelio indicated a room off the elegant portico, away from the excited buzz of the party. I entered, putting my back to the wall and once more lowering my gaze in respect.

I could feel Aelio's heavy regard on me, and when I chanced a glance from beneath my lashes, his brow was furrowed in concentration.

He cleared his throat. "The empire owes you a debt, Miss," he said with polite formality. "Your actions tonight were brave."

"I didn't even think," I lied. "I just saw the dagger and panicked."

Aelio made a humming noise. "I see. Well, if your aim is that good when you're panicking, I'd hate to see what you could accomplish when your head is clear."

"I'm relieved I was able to stop him," I said, radiating innocence. "How frightening it must be to know that random strangers want you dead."

"Vexing, certainly," Aelio replied. "At any rate, I wish to offer you a boon at His Imperial Majesty's behest. Is there anything in particular that you desire? Money? Jewels?"

"Well," I began in a hopeful tone, "I wouldn't say no to a job that doesn't involve inebriated old men pinching my arse all the time."

Aelio let out a little huff that might have been amusement. "That seems like an understandable ambition. I'll have a word with the palace adjunct and see what positions are available. Though I'd strongly suggest saying yes to the money as well — if you don't mind taking a bit of unsolicited advice."

It was my turn to give a little laugh. "Money's good, too. Thanks."

He nodded. "Return to the servants' entrance near the kitchens tomorrow morning when the sun breaches the top of the palace wall. Ask for Madame Fritch, and tell her Tribuni Aelio sent you."

"Thank you," I said, meaning it with all my heart. "I'll definitely do that."

He dipped his chin in acknowledgement. "Good. And now, if you'll forgive me, I suspect the party is already back in full swing. I don't think anyone would blame you if you wanted to call it a night after all the excitement—"

"I'll dance," I told him quickly, exhilaration over my unexpected good fortune thrumming through my veins.

"Very well," Aelio said, indicating the door with an economical gesture of one hand. "With luck, the elderly drunkards will exercise a bit more restraint now that they've seen you take down a man with an oil lamp."

Somehow, I doubted that—but I gave him a sunny smile anyway before retracing my path to the atrium and rejoining the other dancers. As Aelio had predicted, the would-be assassin had already been dragged away, and the revelers were back to their revelry as though nothing had happened.

I spared a thought for the burned man, thanking him silently for giving me the chance I'd needed to gain closer access to the palace... and more specifically, to Emperor Kaeto. I'd been here in the Alyrion capital city of Amarius for almost two months now as a spy, and this was the first time I'd even managed to get inside the same room as the infuriating bastard.

Long time, the voice in my head said wistfully. *Miss you.*

Too long, I agreed. *It's necessary, though.*

The four dragon eggs that had been stolen from my island home of Eburos might already have hatched in the time it had taken me to get this close to my imperial target. The Alyrion Empire had been my people's hereditary enemy for far longer than I'd been alive. The idea that there might be valuable dragon eggs in the emperor's possession was unthinkable.

If Kaeto managed to raise his own dragon army to combat ours, the fragile peace that had held for the past two decades would come crumbling down, plunging the continent once more into war. I had to get those eggs back… and now, I finally had a way inside the stronghold of the man who'd ordered them stolen.

TWO

"**Y**ou've been out of communication for *two months*, Darra." Orlene's tone stayed low and carefully level, which generally meant she was pissed off at me. Even so, the words cut through the background noise of the squalid little tavern like a knife.

I didn't take it to heart, despite the fact that the bulk of those two months since my foray into thwarting assassins had been spent drudging day and night in the palace, trying to get close to an egg-thieving emperor. She'd only been worried for my safety, not that she'd ever admit to such a thing aloud.

"I'm in communication with Xael," I told her—quite reasonably, I thought. "Your dragons would have known if my dragon was upset about anything."

"Or if he was dead," Valeph added under his breath, his distinctive white-blond hair and pale eyes shadowed beneath his hood.

He had a valid point, but we'd known the risks when we came here to retrieve the stolen eggs. Orlene, Valeph, and I were all dragon-bound. It gave us the advantage of fast transportation across the narrow sea separating Eburos from the continent, not to mention a form of mental communion with our mounts that transcended distance. Unfortunately, it also meant that if any of us should die, our bonded dragon would immediately drop dead as well—and vice versa.

We'd left the creatures safely across the border in Utrea before entering Alyrios. Utrea and Eburos were staunch allies, not least because my Eburosi aunt was wed to Utrea's king. Our dragons were under the care of the ruling family, but even from so far away, if Xael had sensed danger to me, the other dragons would have picked up on it and passed on the information to Orlene and Valeph.

And, as Valeph had said, if Xael had randomly died, they'd know I was dead, too.

Lavinio—the only member of our party without his own dragon—cleared his throat. "Maybe we should skip ahead to the part where you tell us what you've found out." He fiddled with his tankard of weak beer, turning it around and around in his grip.

I nodded. We'd chosen this tavern partly because it was disreputable, but mostly because it tended to attract a cross-section of the capital city's lower classes. Even if we hadn't been speaking a pidgin version of northern Eburosi that was unlikely to be understood by strangers, no one else was paying us any attention.

Lavinio and I could easily pass for Alyrion, with our dark brown hair and brown eyes. Valeph and Orlene couldn't say the same. They were both wearing cloaks with the hoods pulled up—Val, to hide his extreme paleness, and Orlene, to cover her red hair. Not that it really mattered. Amarius was a melting pot for people from all over the continent and beyond. Also, the other patrons were far too concerned with their own troubles to worry about what a table of foreign strangers was up to.

"So, I managed to get a job in the palace as a servant," I said. "Which, to be honest, I don't recommend. It's been sheer misery, and just for the record, I hate it."

Orlene eyed me, raising a brow as she leaned back in her chair and crossed muscular arms over her chest. "Aww. Are you getting blisters from the hard work, princess?"

I scowled at her, not about to admit that *yes*, I had blisters. Fun fact—it turned out that sword calluses and calluses from hauling mop buckets around were in completely different places on your hands.

"*Anyway…* last week was the first time they let me have an afternoon off since I started the job," I said. "Which is why it took me so long to get a message to the drop point and set up this meeting. Allegedly, I now have six hours off work at this time every week. I wouldn't rely on it, though. I get the impression it could be revoked at any time and for any reason."

"How did you manage to secure this position?" Valeph asked, a furrow marking his pallid forehead. "I can't imagine they hire people off the street to work at the palace."

"I guess the emperor just liked my face," I said breezily, drawing idle patterns in the condensation on the sticky table.

Valeph's eyes narrowed. "You're lying." He sounded tired, rather than irritated.

I sighed. There wasn't any point in prevaricating when in the presence of our resident magician. Val could sense, without fail, whether the people around him were telling the truth or not. Most people, at least. Lavinio, for instance, was oddly resistant to his powers, a fact which both intrigued and exasperated the former pagan priest.

"The truth? I was acting as a hired dancer at one of Kaeto's posh celebrations when an assassin pulled a knife and tried to sneak past the guards," I admitted. "I… um… *prevented* him."

Valeph winced.

Orlene snorted. "'*Keep a low profile,*' you said. '*It's important we don't draw attention,*' you said."

I glared at her. "It's not like I planned it ahead of time!"

"Well, as long as it worked," Lavinio cut in, neatly heading off the argument. "Next question — have you learned anything useful in two months?"

The words tasted sour in my mouth. "No. Not a single bloody thing."

There hadn't been so much as a hint of gossip among the servants about dragon eggs, dragon hatchlings, or dragon *anything*. And I hadn't had contact with anyone higher up in the imperial hierarchy than the dour Madame Fritch, so servants' gossip was all I had access to.

"Bugger," Orlene muttered.

"It's still our best angle," I said doggedly. "Unless the rest of you have found out anything while I've been stuck in the palace?"

"Nothing useful," Lavinio admitted. "And it's not for lack of trying — believe me."

Gruff, middle-aged Lavinio had come along with us because of his years of experience with hatching dragon eggs and raising the tiny dragonets to adolescence. He'd never bonded with any of his charges, claiming that he preferred to dedicate himself equally to all the hatchlings in his care, rather than focusing on only one dragon. Nevertheless, his experience made him a useful addition to the group... even if it meant he had to ride double with someone when we were traveling by dragonback.

He ran a hand through his perpetually messy hair, his brown eyes meeting mine and holding. "We all know His Imperial Ballsack could have hatched those eggs months ago."

"Yes, I'm well aware," I snapped, not needing the reminder that with this whole operation taking so long, Kaeto might already have hatchlings growing safely in hiding somewhere.

But Lavinio raised a placating hand, palm out. "All I'm saying is, maybe keep an ear out for anyone talking about a wildfire. Hatching those eggs would require a big one. People might notice."

I took a deep breath and let some of the frustration flow out of me. "No, you're right. That's a good idea."

Both Utrea and Eburos had tested several methods for hatching dragon eggs. Bonfires, blacksmith forges... you name it, someone had probably tried it over the years since dragons had returned to the skies. The only thing that had ever worked was starting a forest fire around the cave where the nest had been laid. Maybe someone in the palace would have noticed something like that—and be willing to gossip about it to a random servant girl.

"We'll plan to meet here at the same time next week," I told them, for lack of any better strategy. "But like I said, I can't guarantee I'll be able to make it. If I can't, I'll try to send a message to the usual place, so you'll know. Of course, I might not be able to do that either."

Orlene nodded. "Fine. We'll keep talking to people in the city. We're also scouting out areas with caves and woods where someone might try to keep dragons in secret."

"Except there aren't any places like that," Val added. "Not nearby. Amarius is surrounded by fields and closely managed logging forests."

"For all we know, the Alyrions may not have the first clue how to hatch these eggs," I said, because right now, that felt like our best hope.

"That's true enough," Lavinio agreed.

Val met my eyes. "Whatever the case, you must be careful, Darra. If anyone in the palace suspects you…"

"I'm always careful," I said lightly. "You know me."

His pale gaze said that he knew me all too well, and that he didn't appreciate the casual lie. But our mission was to retrieve those eggs—no matter the cost. Without dragons of their own, our enemies in Alyrios were no match for the combined forces of Utrea and Eburos. With them, the fragile status quo would come tumbling down around our heads.

Careful didn't really come into it.

❧ ♔ ❧

I returned to the palace to find Madame Fritch in a high temper, her wrinkled cheeks flushed red and her iron-gray hair escaping its bun.

"Where have you been, girl?" she demanded.

"It's my afternoon off," I said, resigned to receiving a random dressing-down I didn't deserve.

"Don't talk to me about time off!" Her face grew even redder. "One of His Imperial Majesty's personal serving girls is ill with a fever! And for some reason I wouldn't *presume* to guess, he's requested *you* to replace her!"

I opened my mouth. Snapped it shut. Tried again, because surely getting close to Kaeto couldn't be this easy. "Excuse me?"

Madame Fritch spluttered in outrage. "You heard me! And if you're not in the royal quarters with wine waiting for him when he returns from sparring, it will be both our heads!" She grabbed my shoulders and frog-marched me to an antechamber, pointing at a filmy dress draped over a chair. "Put that on and be quick about it! You're a disgrace to this palace!"

I was happy to be a disgrace to every palace on the continent if it meant getting back in Kaeto's immediate presence. Ignoring the insult, I changed quickly and finger-combed my hair into a semblance of neatness.

Madame Fritch swept me from head to toe and gave a reluctant nod. "You'll do, I suppose. Now, follow me!"

I followed her to Kaeto's royal apartments in the heart of the palace, where two guards stood flanking the double doors. One bowed to Madame Fritch and gestured at me to enter the luxurious room. Once I had, he closed the door unceremoniously in her face.

"Could you show me where the wine is kept?" I asked as meekly as I could manage, then set myself to pouring a goblet once he obliged.

A few minutes later, a young man with a lyre hurried in, giving me a nervous smile. "Hello. You must be the new girl."

"Yes, that's right—" I began, but he ignored me, crossing to an unobtrusive alcove with a single chair in the corner. There, he sat down and began tuning his instrument.

Before I could make another attempt at conversation, the doors opened again. I snapped my jaw shut as Kaeto and Aelio walked in, both of them tousled and sweat damp.

"… an example must be made of them," Kaeto was saying. He unbuckled the sword belt at his waist, ignoring me as he crossed to a shelf and laid it there.

"I understand that, Your Majesty," Aelio replied, coming to a halt inside the door and standing at parade rest. "But the reports of unrest in the outlying areas are growing in frequency and number. Executions may be seen as fuel on the fire rather than—"

He broke off, his attention falling on me as though he'd just realized I was there. I did my best to look vacant and disinterested. Kaeto frowned, following Aelio's gaze to me.

"May I offer you wine, Your Imperial Majesty?" I asked sweetly.

Kaeto's sharp eyes narrowed. "Ah, yes. The firebrand. Leave us now, Aelio. We will speak more on this subject later. Bring me that wine, girl—but taste it first. Not all assassins wield blades, after all. Some wield poison."

THREE

Kaeto's palace had a number of security measures in place to ensure his safety—the occasional random assassin at a party notwithstanding. Working in the background as a servant, I'd seen many of those measures in action firsthand. For that reason, I didn't have too many qualms about lifting the goblet of wine to my lips and taking a couple of healthy swallows.

You had to give the man this much—he clearly appreciated a good vintage. I took a split second to savor the rich, oaky sweetness. Then I crossed to place it on a side table next to the cushioned chair where Kaeto had settled himself. Bowing my head, I pointedly turned the goblet so that his imperial lips wouldn't land in the same place my lowly servant's lips had.

He made no immediate move to drink it, presumably because he was waiting a few minutes to see if I started vomiting uncontrollably or collapsed into violent convulsions. Instead, he began to remove his leather gloves in a deliberate manner, one slow finger at a time. I took in his languid pose with my peripheral vision, not looking directly at his face. The prickle of awareness on my neck told me he wasn't offering me the same courtesy.

"Musician," he said, "play the *Ballad of Armeteza*."

Immediately, the haunting sounds of a lyre in skilled hands filled the elegant room, neither too soft nor too loud.

"You are a dancer, are you not?" Kaeto asked. "When you aren't burning men alive, that is."

As a dragonrider, the irony of the words wasn't lost on me. But on the positive side, I'd apparently made an impression on him. For now, I was more than content to exist in Kaeto's awareness as *'that crazy woman who took out an assassin with an oil lamp.'*

"I am, Your Imperial Majesty," I replied. "Would you like me to dance for you?"

He made a wordless noise that I chose to interpret as an affirmative response. When I risked a full glance at him as I straightened from my respectful bow, it was to find that he'd discarded the gloves next to the wine. His head had fallen back to rest against the cushioned top of the chair, and his eyes were closed.

The overall effect was one of combined exhaustion, tension, and performative indifference to his surroundings. My gaze couldn't help catching on the exposed arch of his throat. His features truly were too sharp to be considered classically handsome, but there was something dangerously appealing about him all the same.

Since I enjoyed keeping my head attached to my shoulders, I made no mention of how wasteful it seemed to ask someone to dance and then not even bother to watch them. I moved silently to the open area at the center of the room, gauging how much space I had to work with, and swept into a simple, flowing series of movements that complemented the mood and tempo of the music.

I was enough of an Eburosi barbarian girl at heart that I would have preferred dancing barefoot to the silken slippers Madame Fritch had dressed me in, but at least the gauzy dress had been designed with freedom of movement in mind. It swirled and wafted around me in a most satisfying way as I lost myself to the physicality of the moment—awaiting whatever happened next.

I'd received many gifts from my dear mother, but a love of dance was perhaps foremost among them. It might have taken twenty-four years before it became a truly important skill in my life—but if Kaeto wanted a servant girl to dance for him, I'd happily do so for hours.

As it happened, it didn't take hours. I watched Kaeto as furtively as I could while I spun and dipped, noting the way the tension gradually eased from his shoulders as music flowed through the imperial chambers. Before long, his striking gray eyes opened, fastening on my movements. I was careful not to examine him too closely after that.

Finally, he let out a slow breath that seemed to come from down around his ankles somewhere. "That will do, musician. You are dismissed."

The flowing notes quieted to a skillful conclusion. I followed them down to stillness, my upper body draped forward over my folded legs, arms artfully outstretched.

"My thanks, Your Imperial Majesty," the musician murmured, and a few moments later, the sound of the chamber door opening and closing reached my ears.

Aside from the nameless, faceless guard standing in the corner of the room—his features obscured by a metal helm—Kaeto and I were alone. I kept my face downturned, my forehead pressed to the luxurious rug… waiting.

"Come, girl," Kaeto said. "Sit by me."

I rose smoothly and crossed to him, cognizant of the notable lack of other chairs nearby. In the absence of other options, I sank down cross-legged on the marble floor at what I judged to be a respectable distance.

"You dance well." Again, I felt the weight of his eyes on me, assessing.

"Thank you, Your Imperial Majesty," I replied, not looking up.

"*Sire* will do in here," Kaeto said. "And you will not be whipped for looking upon my face, girl. What is your name?"

I looked up, relieved, since my neck was starting to develop a crick by this point in the proceedings. "It's Darra, sire," I told him—safe enough, as it was a perfectly common name.

"*Darra*," he repeated, as though tasting the word. "And where exactly do you hail from, Darra Firebrand? Your accent is unfamiliar to me."

That stung a bit, actually—since I'd believed my Alyrion accent to be quite good, thank you very much.

"I grew up in a small village near the southern edge of the Utrean border, sire," I said, my fictional backstory at the ready. "Sydrilla, by name... though I doubt you'd have reason to know of the place."

He gave a hum of acknowledgement and picked up the wine goblet, drinking deep. Apparently, enough time had elapsed without any horrific symptoms on my part for him to trust that the drink wasn't poisoned.

"*Sydrilla*. No, I can't say I've heard of it." He set the wine aside, tilting his head as he examined me. "Would you say the people of your village are happy with their lot in life?"

I hesitated, because I hadn't put a lot of thought into the fictional emotional state of my fictional home village. Frankly, it wasn't the sort of question I'd expected to have to answer.

"I would say that some of them are happy and some of them are not," I replied carefully. "Largely in response to the trials and bounties common to any small settlement reliant on the vagaries of weather and the One God's will. My family was content enough, most of the time."

His gaze on me didn't waver. "And yet, you felt moved to uproot yourself and travel hundreds of leagues to a new city. That doesn't sound like the actions of someone content with her life."

For this, at least, I'd rehearsed an answer. I snorted softly. "It sounded more appealing than staying and marrying the obnoxious prat my parents had promised me to, sire."

He gave a small huff of amusement. "Avowed willfulness is not generally a desirable trait in a servant, you realize."

"Perhaps not," I agreed. "I'm hoping that being a good dancer and occasionally throwing things at would-be assassins is enough to tip the scales in my favor."

At that, he chuckled aloud—the sound low and full-throated.

"I see." He rose from his chair, stretching from side to side to ease his spine. "Now, firebrand, I desire a bath after the torture session that Tribuni Aelio calls sparring." Yet again, he subjected me to that critical, assessing look of his. "Tell me, Darra of Sydrilla—are you a virgin?"

And that was... unexpected.

Maybe it shouldn't have been, though. If there was one thing that irritated me about the northern parts of the continent, it was their bizarre obsession with women being virgins. My response might have been a risky tactical decision on my part, but Kaeto had seemed amused by my *avowed willfulness* a moment ago.

I raised a pointed eyebrow at him. "Such a question, sire. Why? Are *you*?"

Surprise flickered across his features. For the first time, I had the impression he was seeing me as a person, rather than a new possession with which to entertain himself. It was only an instant, and then the cool mask of *emperor* cloaked his expression.

"I wish only to know whether you are likely to shriek and faint at the sight of a nude male body, girl," he said. "As I see that you are not, you may attend me. Come, then. I grow weary of my own filth."

I rose and followed him to the attached bathing room without comment, wondering idly if the title of imperial serving girl was expected to come with sexual favors attached. Even though I assumed such a man would be an entitled prick about sex, I couldn't say I was actively *averse* to the idea. He really was *surprisingly* easy on the eyes.

With more curiosity than trepidation, I trailed into the lavish marble room off the main chambers, readying myself to disrobe and bathe the ruler of an empire. In the back of my mind, a distant dragon rolled his eyes at me, long-suffering.

Pretty doesn't mean safe, Xael sent through the bond.

That's all right, I sent back. *We both know safe is boring.*

FOUR

It wasn't a terribly surprising development when the guard followed us into the emperor's bathing chamber. I might have acted to stop a random assassin at a party, but even after two months, I remained a largely unknown quantity within the palace. A man like Kaeto didn't stay alive in a city like Amarius by blindly trusting every new person who came his way.

Other servants had been at work behind the scenes to ready Kaeto's bath. The white-tiled floor led down to a sunken tub set in the center of the room. It was full and waiting, steam rising from the water in gentle curls. Rose petals floated on the surface like drops of crimson blood.

"Well? Undress me, then," Kaeto said, with a ruler's impatience. "Even *I* am becoming offended by my stench." He shifted his shoulders restlessly, as though trying to work kinks out of his spine. "Some evenings, I'm convinced Aelio uses our training sessions as an excuse to gain revenge for whatever petty slights are irking him that day."

The faintest snort of amusement emerged from behind the guard's featureless vizor. Kaeto turned a sharp glare in the man's direction, and he abruptly went as still as a statue in his post by the door.

I turned my attention to the buckles and fastenings holding Kaeto's clothing closed, thinking wryly of all the abuse I'd taken over the years from various weapons masters in the name of training. One did not learn adequate skills in self-defense without gaining bruises along the way. Apparently, not even emperors were an exception to that rule.

As I peeled off Kaeto's sweat-stained linen shirt, it revealed a purpling mark blooming on his left shoulder, and a second one low on the right side of his ribs. The faded remains of a handful of other marks decorated his torso. None were serious. All were proof that Aelio cared more for his ruler's skill with a sword than the state of his pristine imperial hide.

Given what I'd heard from my sources about the loyal palace tribuni, that didn't come as a surprise. It did, however, go a long way toward explaining Kaeto's reputation for being a decent fighter, despite having seen little in the way of real battle.

He certainly had the physique for it. That became more obvious, the more clothing I removed. The emperor was naturally pale-skinned, and even with the excess of fine food and drink available to him at a snap of his fingers, there wasn't an ounce of fat anywhere on the man.

He was wiry rather than broad. Muscle and sinew stood out in ropy cords on his forearms and biceps. His chest and shoulders narrowed to a trim waist above slender hips. When I matter-of-factly removed his boots and pulled down his breeches, I was treated to the sight of a taut and shapely arse in profile as he twisted to step out of them.

I couldn't help a quick glance at his cock, because why not? I mean... how often did a girl get a glimpse of an imperial prick, after all? It hung quiescent among a thatch of dark curls. A good size, long and slender like the rest of him—but otherwise completely unremarkable.

All in all, he reminded me of the long-limbed coursing dogs popular with the nobles in Utrea. Beautiful to look at—but also nervy, high-strung, and prone to snapping at people unexpectedly. Without a word, he turned and stepped into the sunken bath, settling himself down with a sigh and spreading his arms along the marble lip. His eyes slipped shut once more, his nostrils flaring as he breathed in the fragrant steam.

I gathered up the discarded clothing and folded it neatly, placing it on a chair next to the door, opposite the unmoving guard. Scanning the room, I located soap, a pitcher, and a soft, woven cloth lying near the tub.

"Shall I wash you, sire?" I asked.

"That *is* why you're here, firebrand," Kaeto replied, without bothering to open his eyes.

Bathing another person was something with which I had surprisingly little experience. I'd been an only child, so I'd never had to wash the dirt off sticky younger siblings. And while the number of lovers I'd had over the years was... not insignificant, bathing them had always fallen into the nebulous and incomprehensible territory of emotional intimacy. A subject in which I was, and always had been, completely incompetent.

On the other hand, how difficult could it be?

I knelt at the edge of the tub and wet the cloth, then swiped it through the jar of soft, sandalwood-scented soap. It couldn't be much different from washing myself, although I did try to play up the sensuality of the act as I rubbed the washcloth over the slope of Kaeto's tense shoulders and hard-muscled chest.

I still had no idea if sexual favors were an expected part of my new role as female body servant to a powerful man. But when I stretched down to rub the soapy cloth over the tops of Kaeto's thighs, letting the edge slide innocently along his cock, the leader of the largest empire the world had ever known knocked my hand away, the movement quick as a striking snake.

In my peripheral vision, I saw the guard tense at the sudden splash of water. I backed off immediately, bowing my head in contrition.

"Forgive me, sire. You do not wish me to pleasure you? When you asked about my sexual experience, I assumed you wanted—"

"No." Gray eyes pinned me. "You'll forgive me if I'm not eager to let someone who burned a man alive handle my cock on such short acquaintance."

Bad tactics, Darra. A stupid mistake to make.

"Of course not, sire. I humbly beg your forgiveness for my presumption."

Kaeto retrieved the fallen rag and took up his own ablutions. His eyes never left me, while his expression grew speculative.

Did the bloody man never blink?

"If you are so eager to prove your worldliness, firebrand, then put your fingers to work on yourself. Since you're so eager, I'm more than content to observe from a distance."

And... *yeah*. I hadn't seen that one coming, either. Once again, he'd surprised me.

There were potential pitfalls here. I'd already noted the value Alyrions placed on so-called feminine purity. On the one hand, I wasn't sure what my acquiescence to putting on a public show for Kaeto and his guard would mean for my reputation in the palace. On the other hand, the Alyrion emperor had just ordered me to do it.

In the end, I was only a servant, as far as anyone here was concerned. I didn't have much of a reputation to start with.

On a personal level, I couldn't care less if they wanted to ogle me while I got myself off. Hell... it could even be fun, under the right circumstances. I'd always had a bit of an exhibitionist streak. But I was still playing a role here, and that role wasn't 'slutty island barbarian girl.'

I looked uncertainly toward the guard. "Sire. We're... not alone."

He raised an eyebrow. "Interesting that this fact wasn't a concern for you when you were preparing to handle me without my permission."

Which was a fair point, damn him.

"Well, I—" I stammered, trying to channel the fictional village girl I was supposed to be. "I didn't realize—"

Kaeto was still watching me with that faintly predatory expression. "You might wish to consider the following fact. Should it circulate among the barracks that you are my latest dalliance, no one else in the palace will dare molest you. Not unless they're in a hurry to be tortured to death over a period of weeks."

The guard had once again gone very still. I wasn't sure he was even breathing. He had the air of someone hoping that if he emulated a piece of statuary effectively enough, it would somehow make him functionally invisible.

"You do make a compelling argument, sire," I allowed. Again, I glanced toward the guard. "But I don't suppose he could, you know—leave first?"

"No," Kaeto said, with a hint of cruelty tingeing his amusement. "I don't suppose he could. However, I assure you he's more than capable of keeping his eyes where they belong."

He leaned back in the bath, regarding me openly. And this should *not* be getting me going as much as it was. But as I'd told Xael through the bond... safe was boring.

I'd always *despised* being bored.

"He'd better, if he knows what's good for him," I said, glaring at the guard to drive home my point.

Neither of them needed to know that these weren't even the strangest circumstances under which I'd masturbated in front of other people.

Though, to be fair, most of the other times had involved some combination of strong wine and hallucinogens.

"You're missing out, you know," I told the emperor of half the continent as I tugged a breast free of my gauzy dress and started teasing it. "I was going to make it really good for you."

Kaeto let out a derisive snort as I arranged myself artfully nearby.

It was a different kind of dance, but I still tried to make it a show as I slid a hand between my legs. And, because I was me—and one should never waste a good climax—there was no question of faking it. Danger had always been my aphrodisiac of choice. Well, danger and that weird brownish-purple spice Val had brought back from one of the northern tribes a couple of years ago.

That shit was *amazing*.

Still, it was driving me a little bit crazy not being able to tell if I was affecting Kaeto. He certainly wasn't touching himself; just watching me from beneath hooded eyelids. Was he hard beneath the water? What kind of game was he playing here?

I came sharply around my fingers, thinking of the vulnerable arch of Kaeto's throat as he lay dozing in his chair earlier. I cried out as my muscles clenched and released, then lay panting as the tension leached from my body, leaving me limp and spent on the polished floor.

"Very nice," Kaeto said in a tone of polite indifference. He sounded like someone attending an amateur theater performance. I half expected him to start slow-clapping.

Instead, a small splashing sound reached my ears. I peeled open one eyelid to find him rising from the bath, clearly unaffected by my shameless display as he reached for a towel and wrapped it around his waist.

"You are dismissed for the evening," he continued. "I will call for you again when I require you."

I stared at him for a blank moment, aware that asking *'wait, what in the gods' names just happened here?'* would probably be a good way to get beheaded, or at least flogged.

"Yes, sire," I muttered, pulling my clothing to rights. With no other options, I clambered to my feet and slunk past the guard without looking at him.

I was pretty sure he was smirking at me behind his steel visor.

☙ ♛ ❧

I spent the next two days obsessing over whether the emperor of Alyrios preferred men, or whether he was one of those people who preferred no one at all when it came to sex. Or perhaps he liked women, but he specifically didn't like *me*.

Then I reminded myself firmly that it didn't matter, because I was apparently his new plaything now. I was here to get close to him, not to seduce him. I went about my duties and kept my head down, waiting to see what would happen next.

On the fourth night, he summoned me again.

He made no mention of our previous evening together, nor did he take a bath. I merely served him wine, danced for him, answered more seemingly random questions about the nonexistent village of Sydrilla, and left when he dismissed me after about an hour.

On the holy day at the end of the week, I gathered my cloak in preparation for my planned rendezvous with Orlene, Valeph, and Lavinio in the city. I was attempting to decide what I could safely tell them—without sounding either incompetent or deranged—when I nearly ran headfirst into Madame Fritch.

"Where in Deimok's name do you think you're going, girl?" she demanded.

"It's my afternoon off…?" I reminded her, my stomach already sinking.

"Are you completely daft, you little fool?" she snapped. "You're one of *the emperor's personal servants* now. You aren't allowed to just swan out of the palace on your own!"

"I'm not?" I asked blankly.

"Of course not!" she said. "Good lord, girl. Do you have no understanding of how sensitive your position is? You can't be privy to His Imperial Majesty's personal business and then go blabbing it to who-knows-who in the city!"

I stared at her. "So, I'm basically a prisoner in the palace now? Seriously?"

She gazed heavenward, as though seeking divine patience. "Don't be so dramatic. Now get back to work before I box your ears. There's cutlery that needs polishing in the kitchens."

Not having any other real options, I turned around and retraced my steps, painfully aware that I now had no way to meet with my comrades. I also had no way to send them a message explaining the new situation.

If you were like me, you could flap your wings and fly away, offered the grumbly presence in my head.

Not helpful, Xael, I sent back.

My dragon only gave a mental shrug in reply.

FIVE

It took the better part of another week to sweet-talk one of the stableboys into delivering a message to the city for me. There was risk in the gambit, to be sure. I doubted the lad's loyalty to a pretty servant girl he'd only met a few days ago would stand up to much in the way of pressure, should he be caught and questioned about his actions.

The note was written in pidgin Eburosi, relying heavily on symbols and pictograms since written language had only come to my island home a few decades earlier. Most educated people there used the Alyrion language for written communications, ironically enough. That meant my native scribbles should be obscure enough on their own. I'd also kept things vague to the point of near uselessness, trusting my comrades to read between the lines.

I was sorry I'd missed our planned meal together… I'd received a highly desirable new position that meant I needed to stay in the palace until further notice. But I was *so happy* for my unexpected good fortune, and I hoped they would be, too.

They'd figure it out, I was fairly certain.

With luck, the money I'd paid my unwitting go-between would motivate him to follow through and drop the little vellum scroll at the designated communication point like I'd asked him to. I didn't really have a way to follow up and confirm it, unfortunately.

Back home on the Kaeto front, things were progressing at a snail's pace. And that was being generous.

I couldn't seem to figure out his angle. Not that I was an expert in getting inside people's heads; that was more Val's specialty.

In some ways, it was a pity our walking truth detector's unusual looks made him a poor candidate for blending into the background as a palace spy. However, the truth was that I hadn't wanted it to be anyone other than me.

If I got myself killed during this mission, it would be my own foolish fault. If someone else got killed while under my command, it would eat at me for the rest of my days. I could practically hear old Caius lecturing me on the importance of using one's assets to their full advantage during wartime. But the Caius-in-my-head could go hang, because this wasn't a war.

Not yet.

Besides, it wasn't as though any of the others could have ended up this close to Kaeto without arousing suspicion. I *was* making progress, even if it didn't feel like it.

The emperor continued to summon me at regular intervals, occasionally multiple times a day. No one in the servants' hall seemed to be talking about the sick girl I'd replaced. I hoped she hadn't died of her fever.

Or been poisoned.

Or been thrown into the palace dungeon.

Or disappeared under mysterious circumstances, never to be seen again.

Needless to say, I didn't ask.

That evening, Kaeto stalked in with the air of someone exhausted by a day of being surrounded by idiots.

"Wine, sire?" I asked, bowing over the cup I extended to him.

"She's already tasted it, Your Majesty," said the ever-present guard.

Kaeto grunted and accepted the offered cup, tipping it up and taking several swallows as I straightened.

"How may I ease your day?" I asked, because I was all-in on this serving girl thing, and I needed to find the key that would further unlock Kaeto's trust in me.

He thrust the wine back in my hand and waved me toward his favorite chair. I set the cup on the table next to it and sank cross-legged to the floor nearby, well-used to this by now. I watched as he unclasped his royal cloak and swept it off his shoulders, depositing the rich fabric over the back of a chaise near the door.

He crossed to the chair and sank down on it with a weary sigh.

"Distract me, firebrand," he said listlessly. "Tell me more about your village."

Over the past couple of weeks, I'd spent an inordinate amount of time and mental energy composing the fictional life of Sydrilla and its inhabitants. So far, I'd managed to avoid contradicting myself or spouting anything too implausible.

This was where growing up in a family of storytellers came in handy.

"Of course, sire," I said. "What would you like to know?"

He let his head fall back, gazing at the ornate ceiling. "Tell me a childhood memory. One that still feels as vivid as when it happened."

The idea popped into my head fully formed. I would have been crazy not to try it.

I licked my lips. "A memory. *Hmm*. When I was twelve, I was playing with my friends on the banks of the river. I looked up, and there was a dragon flying low in the western sky. Its scales were the color of rubies... of blood. It was the most beautiful and terrifying thing I'd ever seen."

In the back of my mind, Xael huffed. I could tell he was secretly pleased by the adjectives I'd chosen, though. *Beautiful* and *terrifying* suited him from his nose to the tip of his amethyst tail.

Kaeto roused himself to look down at me. I gazed up at him from beneath lowered lashes.

"I've thought of dragons often since then," I said. "Just imagine how the world would change if Alyrios had its own dragon army."

Kaeto's gaze on me was cool. "Imagine how the world would change?" he echoed. "Why, that's simple enough. There would be a war to end all wars, and when it was finally done, the cartographers would have to redraw all their maps."

A faint chill shivered down my spine. *He knows*, I thought. *The spies were right. Kaeto is behind the theft of the eggs, and he wants to wipe Eburos and Utrea off the face of the world.*

"I'm sure you're right," I managed. "Do you think it will ever happen?"

His cool expression never wavered. "Who can say? Perhaps it will, one day."

This was closer to my goal than I'd ever come before, but Kaeto wasn't exactly going to come out and tell me he had four dragon eggs hidden in the foothills. As much as I wanted to, I didn't dare push the subject any further.

"So, what about you, sire?" I asked. "What's your most vivid childhood memory?"

Kaeto's face remained unreadable, and he was silent for long enough that I worried I'd overstepped.

"I was nine years old," he said, "and I'd just realized that my older brother was a sadistic monster. A sadistic monster who would one day rule the Alyrion Empire—if I didn't do something about it first."

I bit down hard on '*So, sadism runs in the family, then?*'

I already knew that it did.

"I'm sorry," I offered. "That must have been an awful thing to face at such a young age."

He waved a hand as though batting my words away. At his gesture, the strange intensity in the room's atmosphere dissipated.

"Had I appreciated the amount of tiresome peacocking involved in rulership, I might've walked away and wished him joy of it," Kaeto said. "Which reminds me, I will shortly be required to travel to the shipyards in Heleva to christen the first of a new class of warship. You will travel with me... in case I have need of entertainment while we camp."

"As you command, sire," I said, dipping my head to hide the way my thoughts had started racing.

Heleva was a river port several days' ride to the south. The overland route traversed rough territory through the mountains, sparsely populated and largely unsuited for agriculture. During the winter, most people who had the means would make such a journey by boat. But during the summer, the biting insects made river travel through the lowlands nearly unbearable.

I had no doubt that Kaeto would be riding with a large retinue for protection. But the fact remained that he would be far more vulnerable outside of the palace walls than inside them.

And... I would be with him. A dragonrider, whose mount could find her anywhere using their bond. A dragon could swoop down on a guard escort and throw a camp into disarray with a single burst of flame from above.

Xael stirred with interest in the depths of my thoughts.

So, how would you feel about abducting an emperor and threatening to flambé him unless he tells us where he's got the dragon eggs stashed? I asked silently, aware of how crazy the idea sounded.

Dragons couldn't smile, but the slow wash of satisfaction through the bond conveyed Xael's feelings just as clearly.

SIX

Fortunately, I'd had several days to refine my plan of '*kidnap Kaeto and threaten him until he tells me everything.*' The original iteration had included a couple of glaring flaws, the main one being that it would immediately spark a war with the Alyrion Empire.

That one was, surprisingly, the easiest to remedy. My stableboy-slash-messenger had proven himself trustworthy—at least so far. When I'd sent him with a follow-up message a few days after the first, he'd returned with a note the others had left for me at the drop-off point.

It wasn't terribly helpful or illuminating; the rough translation essentially consisting of '*Great, fabulous… well done, you. Now what the hell are the rest of us supposed to do?*' I hadn't had a good answer at the time. Now, I did.

My next message was more difficult to compose, simply because being ridiculously vague wasn't going to cut it for this. I'd have to rely on the impenetrability of written Eburosi to the average Alyrion citizen and hope for the best.

Return to the others, I wrote. *Tell my aunt to spread the message of a rogue barbarian warrior girl who escaped with a you-know-what and is acting on her own, without official sanction from the Tribal Council. Have her contact my family and get them to spread the same story from Eburos.*

I could only imagine the creative cursing Orlene would come up with in response to the orders to return to Utrea and reunite with their dragons, or the way Val would shake his head and cover his face in despair. I thought maybe Lavinio would understand the necessity, though. I was more than willing to throw myself under the wheels of the metaphorical wagon if it meant getting those dragon eggs back.

Or, in a pinch, destroying them. Doing so would rip my heart from my chest, but I would destroy the eggs as a last resort before I let Alyrios have them.

Distress flooded the dragon bond, and my heart twisted further. Xael didn't understand—or care—about human territorial politics. Frankly, I envied him that indifference. He understood good hunting and the joy of flight. He understood loyalty and adventure and the satisfaction of a healthy clutch of dragonets in the weyr.

If it came to crushing the eggs, I'd have to do it myself. And then, it was very possible I'd find out what it was like to be soul-bound to a creature who was furious with me.

Hopefully, it wouldn't come to that. There weren't so many dragons in the world that we could afford to lose four of them. My plan was to grab Kaeto, try to get the information from him, and use Xael to force my way into wherever the eggs were being kept so I could retrieve them safe and intact. I even had a backup plan in place—if threatening Kaeto directly didn't work, I'd pretend to be part of an imaginary Alyrion faction and try to ransom him in exchange for the eggs.

Either way, Xael could outdistance any pursuit by land or sea. I'd head east, away from both Utrea and Eburos, then fly the eggs to my island home only after throwing the Alyrions off our scent.

The remaining important question was whether to kill Kaeto or leave him alive. If I left him alive, there was no guarantee he wouldn't try to steal dragons again in the future. But if I killed him, it wasn't at all clear who would take his place, and whether we'd be better or worse off than before.

You like him, said the unhelpful presence in my head.

That doesn't really come into it, I shot back.

⤙ ♛ ⤚

The day of our departure dawned gray and windy. I was happy to be an afterthought—barely more than another piece of luggage in the imperial retinue. It gave me a chance to observe.

There were surprisingly few servants accompanying the entourage. Fewer than half a dozen, and that included the ones responsible for wrangling the pack animals. A cook. A few grooms. And little old me, the emperor's new toy. Combined with Kaeto, the three dozen soldiers forming his imperial guard, Tribuni Aelio, and a couple of hangers-on from court, the entire group numbered less than fifty.

I was relying on my memorization of the Alyrion maps that had been available in my home city of Rhyth, combined with the chatter among the retinue, to plan my attack.

You mean my *attack*, Xael grumbled.

I ignored him, eyeing the little ambling pony I was expected to ride.

Looks tasty, Xael offered. *Slow and easy to catch.*

He was needling me for a reaction, which tended to be what happened when a battle-dragon spent too long stuck in an unfamiliar weyr without anything to do except offer snide mental commentary to his absent rider.

Don't eat horses, please, I replied, refusing to be baited. *Even slow ones.*

The pony sneezed, spraying me with a fine mist of snot.

"I could reconsider," I told it evenly.

It shook its head, sending the bridle's hardware jingling.

At least I wasn't expected to ride double behind a soldier. Madame Fritch had outfitted me with a modest split skirt that accommodated riding astride, and someone had thoughtfully covered the saddle with a thick layer of sheepskin to save my delicate dancer's thighs. Never mind that those dancer's thighs had straddled a dragon during daylong patrols over the Southern Sea on a regular basis for several years now.

To be fair to them, this journey wouldn't be an easy ride—slow-gaited ambler or no. We would start off traveling parallel to, but upland of the river that ran south from the port city of Amarius. On the third day, we'd veer east to reach the closest pass through the mountains that separated northern Alyrios from the more southerly river port that was our destination.

The River Uvi had carved a path through those mountains over the eons. But travel upstream by water was slow, and river-goers risked contracting swamp fever from the massive swarms of biting insects endemic to the area during the summer.

That worked out perfectly for me. My mentor Caius—who'd been an Alyrion soldier for decades before running afoul of the imperial family and escaping to Eburos—had traveled these mountains many times. He'd drilled me on Alyrion geography for weeks before this mission had started, and I had a pretty good idea of where to stage my imperial abduction.

The pass we'd be traversing wove through broken land that included a dry canyon barely wide enough for six horses to ride abreast. Once the column rode into that canyon, they'd be easy pickings for a dragon on the wing. All I needed to do was get close to Kaeto as we entered the ravine and call Xael in after us. With the soldiers in disarray, I was pretty sure I could overpower Kaeto, who wouldn't expect me to pose a threat.

It sounded simple enough. Separate him from the rest of the column, at knifepoint if necessary, and wait for Xael to land nearby, holding the guards at bay with his fiery breath. The narrow gorge would make it a squeeze for Xael to take off again while carrying two people, but I was confident he could do it.

Easy.

Xael snorted.

What? I can't help it if I'm a natural optimist, I told him, and swung up to sit in the pony's saddle.

The first two days were the same combination of boredom, tedium, and inconvenience as all overland journeys tended to be. The pack mule train ensured that even on the well-traveled flatlands south of the capital, our speed was limited to a slow plod. This probably made my borrowed mount happy, since plodding seemed to be his natural speed.

On the first and second nights, we stayed in decently sized towns along the route, where the inn owners stumbled over themselves to provide hospitality and good food for the imperial retinue. I bathed Kaeto in the evenings and dressed him in the mornings, but beyond that, he apparently hadn't felt the need for my *entertainment*, as he'd put it.

The third day saw us parting ways with the river route, and with it, most signs of civilization. I hadn't been certain what sort of travel the mountain pass saw at this time of year. The answer was some, but not much. We occasionally met trade caravans coming from the other direction, but they were small and infrequent as the day rolled on. They inevitably gave us a wide berth—not that I could blame them, with the soldiers' bristling weapons.

I held my breath, but none of them came running over to us to blather about having seen a riderless dragon wheeling in the sky.

I'd called on Xael to fly in from Utrea first thing that morning. I told him to find an inconspicuous place to hide among the peaks looming above the northernmost ravine along the pass—well out of sight of any passing riders, but only a couple minutes' flight away from where I would need him at the canyon entrance.

As the sun passed its zenith, the terrain around us grew craggier, and my nerves grew taut with anticipation.

Be ready, I sent, as the slopes on either side of the trail closed in, steepening to sheer walls ahead.

Kaeto was riding with Aelio and two courtiers in the center of the column, while I rode with the other servants toward the back. The mule train was behind us, followed by a small rear guard of six soldiers.

I relayed this to Xael, intending to have him strike as the guards in front of the small servant group entered the ravine—splitting the column and panicking the pack mules. This would hopefully remove the six rear guards from the equation as they tried to deal with the confusion of escaping animals outside of the canyon's confines.

It really was a perfect place for an ambush. As the front of the column approached the entrance, I kicked the pony into a faster gait, pasting a resolute look onto my face.

"Excuse me," I said, weaving past the soldiers' larger horses as I headed for the center of the group. "Excuse me. I need to speak to Tribuni Aelio—It's urgent."

The soldiers I passed scowled at me, and one called, "Hey there, girl! Get back with the other servants!" But none of them physically tried to stop me.

I reached my targets just as we entered the enclosed walls of stone. *Ready,* I warned Xael, and was aware of him leaping from his perch, his great wings spread wide.

"Tribuni Aelio!" I called. "Forgive me, sir—but it's urgent. There's a problem among the servants..."

Both Aelio and Kaeto turned to look at me, frowning in confusion. Before I could draw breath to come up with some other nonsense to spout, a jolt of alarm echoed through the bond.

Unknown riders, Xael sent sharply. *Too many! Descending the slope behind you!*

I had a moment to think *'what the actual fuck?',* followed by a flash of realization.

It really was the perfect place for an ambush.

Apparently, I wasn't the only person who'd thought so. Well, *shit.*

The distant echo of thundering hoofbeats, muffled by the stone walls surrounding us, filtered to my ears past the familiar sounds of the column.

Change of plan, I told Xael, just as the first shouts of, "Ambush! *It's a trap!"* erupted from the soldiers forming the rear guard.

SEVEN

"There are armed riders descending from the mountains behind us!" I shouted, immediately ditching my original *there's a problem with the servants* angle and hoping everyone would be too distracted to pick up on it.

Both Aelio and Kaeto fastened their attention upon me like hawks preparing to dive for the kill.

"How many?" Aelio demanded, all business.

"Couldn't count them," I said breathlessly. "Lots, though. Too many."

"Too bad we don't have any oil lamps for you to throw at them." Kaeto's tone was waspish, but he transferred the reins of his fine buckskin stallion to his left hand and drew his sword with his right.

"No time for banter," Aelio barked. "We'll try to outdistance them through the ravine while the guards hold the rear. You six!" He pointed toward the milling guards closest to us. "Lead the way! Ride as hard as you can without breaking a horse's leg!"

Trying to outrun the riders behind us was a desperate gambit. Any organized attack worth its salt would have more riders waiting ahead of us to cut off our escape, and Aelio had to know that as well as I did. But there were only two directions to go, and the echo of screams and clashing steel was already approaching us from behind.

Aelio swept his gaze over the two aging courtiers in the group before it landed on me. "Keep up. We can't slow down for you."

I returned a curt nod and spurred my pony forward as Aelio and Kaeto wheeled, galloping after the guards. The pony gave a startled crowhop in response to the press of my heels before launching itself past the courtiers' larger horses, hot in pursuit of my quarry.

It was like riding a very small and very unhappy earthquake, but 'short' didn't always equate to 'slow.' The pony had a surprising turn of speed, although endurance might be another matter entirely. Behind us, the courtiers' panicked cries of *"Wait!"* and *"Slow down!"* were already growing fainter.

The pair would realize soon enough that Aelio hadn't been lying. As the Amarian palace tribuni, his only concern was for the safety of his emperor. The rest of us would have to keep pace with them or be sacrificed to the larger goal of protecting the empire's ruler.

The pony's hooves skidded on shale, and I grabbed mane as the animal bobbled alarmingly before righting itself.

Stick to riding dragons, muttered the presence in my head, as the pony recovered in time to hurtle over a poorly placed boulder in the path. *It's safer.*

Not helpful, I sent back. *Why are you never helpful when I'm in situations like this?*

Sure enough, we'd barely gone half a league when Aelio let out a sharp curse. He and Kaeto were perhaps five horse-lengths ahead of me, but I could hear the same thing he must have heard—a cacophony of hooves echoing against the canyon's high walls. Far too many to be the forward guards' horses—and they were growing louder.

Aelio held up his hand for a halt. I reined in the fractious pony, barely avoiding crashing into Kaeto's lathered mount.

That put me close enough to hear Aelio's murmured, "I'm so sorry, sire," before he drew steel and bellowed, "Protect the emperor!" The six guards shouted a ragged battle cry, following their commander as he charged toward the unknown danger with his sword held high.

Kaeto's face might have been carved from the same stone as the ravine. I drew breath to speak, only to be interrupted by the noisy arrival of one of the lagging courtiers. Of the other one, there was no sign. He might have fallen, or perhaps he'd panicked and turned back when he heard the fresh threat approaching from the canyon in front of us.

It didn't matter.

"You might want to get off your horse now," I told him, suiting action to word as I dismounted and let the pony run loose.

"What?" panted the old man, clutching his reins in white-knuckled fingers.

"Get back on that pony, firebrand!" Kaeto snapped. "What are you doing?"

I ignored him, grabbing the buckskin's reins in one hand and the hem of Kaeto's ornate tunic in the other.

Come and get us, please, I told Xael, jerking the stallion's head around at the same time I yanked with all my strength, dragging the startled emperor from the saddle. Kaeto crashed to the ground with a shout, his sword flying free of his hand. I kicked the weapon out of range and stepped back before he could recover enough of his wits to try and take me down with him.

"Stop, stop!" bleated the useless courtier. "*Traitor!*"

"Not exactly," I told him, as the rush of unnatural wind whipped at the escaping tendrils of my hair. "To be a traitor, I'd have to be Alyrion. And just for the record, I did warn you to dismount while you had the chance."

Great wings thumped through the air above us. The buckskin stallion and the pony panicked and bolted, heading back the way we'd come. The courtier's mount screamed in terror and reared as its rider wrestled with the reins. Its hind hooves slipped and scrabbled on the rocks, sending it crashing backward to the ground. It flailed for a moment before regaining its feet and galloping after its herdmates, leaving the broken body of the crushed courtier behind. Blood spread slowly outward from beneath the man's head, in an ever-expanding crimson puddle.

A great amethyst-colored dragon dropped into the canyon in front of us, looming over the still-winded Kaeto. He'd made it partway upright, balanced on a hand and a knee as he gasped for breath, but at the sight of the scaly creature looming over him with its serpentine neck, gimlet eyes, and razor-sharp teeth, he fell onto his rump and started trying to crab-crawl backward, away from Xael's beady regard.

I let Kaeto run into my legs, halting his frantic scramble. I doubted he was even aware I was still here. He gasped and craned around, taking in my utter lack of concern about the massive dragon menacing us. I pulled the wicked little paring knife I'd liberated from the palace kitchens out of its hiding place in my belt and dragged Kaeto to his feet, pressing the blade to his throat.

Behind us, a thunder of hoofbeats approached from the direction of the first attack—the one that had come from the mountain slopes.

"You've got two choices, Your Imperial Majesty," I said. "Don't worry, though—this is an easy one. You can either come with me, or you can die where you stand."

EIGHT

I had to give Kaeto credit. He stared at me for a beat, then he stared at the dragon eyeballing him with an inscrutable expression that might have meant anything from '*This is boring*' to '*I wonder how you'd taste barbecued.*' Next, Kaeto's sharp gray eyes scanned our immediate surroundings—empty of other people if you didn't count the body of the elderly courtier.

The usual reaction to the sudden appearance of a dragon was panic. I could see the emperor shoving that panic aside in favor of the kind of practicality that would save his life.

"This beast is yours, firebrand?" he asked, as though to confirm it.

"What do you mean? No, we've never met before," I quipped, because people who stated the blindingly obvious were tiresome.

His eyes narrowed. It was a look that said flogging might have been involved if we'd been back at the palace. Unfortunately for him, we weren't at the palace—and he had no guards, no useful weapons, and a small army bearing down on him that apparently meant business.

"I choose to go with you, in that case," he said. "Though I suppose I see now where your penchant for burning people alive comes from."

"See? I told you it was an easy choice," I replied. "Xael?"

The dragon huffed a billow of smoke and lowered his bulk onto the canyon floor.

I tugged Kaeto over to his shoulder and stuck the paring knife back in my belt. Weaving my fingers together to form a stirrup, I jerked my chin to indicate he should let me help him onto Xael's back.

"If future imperial heirs are a concern, make sure to find a place to sit that isn't pointy," I counseled, hefting him up like I was giving him a leg-up onto a horse.

Kaeto snarled a curse as he apparently landed someplace that *was* pointy, then he shifted back a few inches to a better position. I let Xael give me a boost up with his scaly snout, taking a seat behind the emperor—because I sure as hell wasn't going to give him my unguarded back.

"You might want to hold on to something," I told him, as enemy riders rounded the canyon bend behind us.

Taking my own advice, I gripped tight with my knees. Xael reared up and launched himself into the air, his body lurching beneath us as powerful wings caught the stiff breeze flowing through the canyon.

The dragon's muscles twisted and bunched as he navigated the narrow ravine, and I silently cursed the unfortunate logistical challenges that meant he had no saddle. I was confident enough of my own ability to stay on, but it would be more than a little awkward if the emperor of Alyrios fell off and went *splat* while I was trying to kidnap him.

Figuring the likelihood that he'd pull a hidden dagger and stab me through the hand was acceptably low, I wrapped one arm around Kaeto's chest from behind. Reaching past him with my other hand, I grasped a conveniently placed chitinous spine and anchored us both in place as best I could.

Kaeto stiffened, but he had more sense than to protest this gross insult to his imperial personage under the circumstances. Beneath my hand, his heart thundered like the receding hoofbeats of the approaching riders far beneath us.

Maybe it was stupid of me, but I guided Xael along the path of the ravine rather than immediately veering back up to the mountain peaks. In my defense, the riders approaching from the rear had already seen us. A huge amethyst dragon crouching in the center of the canyon wasn't exactly something you could miss... or mistake.

Aelio had been a staunch friend to my mentor, Caius, before Caius had fallen afoul of court politics and been forced to flee Alyrios. I'd have had a hard time ever looking the old imperial commander in the eye again if I fled without checking on his comrade's fate.

None of the troops below us would be armed with dragon harpoons. There was no reason they *would* be, and anyway, those infernal war machines were far too unwieldy for terrain like this. It would be safe enough, and it wouldn't give the attacking forces any information they didn't already have. They'd seen us. They knew that Kaeto had escaped on dragonback.

The imperial guards and the second group of attackers had clashed less than half a league ahead of us. The first flyover only offered an impression of violent confusion, though it was clear that Aelio's forces had been quickly overpowered.

When we circled back, slowing to a glide, more details became evident. Half a dozen men had converged on a magnificent bay courser that lay downed on its side, its legs flailing weakly. They were pulling a limp figure free from the animal's saddle.

Kaeto drew in a sharp breath, his chest rising jerkily beneath my hand.

Several people on the ground started shouting, pointing up at us and gesturing excitedly. Then jagged rock walls cut off my view once more. I was pretty sure I'd recognized the unfortunate bay horse, but Kaeto's reaction confirmed it.

"Take us down!" he shouted, the words blown back to me on the wind.

"Not a chance!" I shouted, veering Xael farther up the mountain slope—as I probably should have done from the beginning.

I felt Kaeto's answering growl more than I heard it, but he wasn't exactly in the best position to impose his will on the situation. Sure, Xael could have gone down there and flash-fried everyone. But Aelio was right in the middle of a knot of enemy fighters, and it wouldn't be practical to transport a third person on dragonback — much less someone who was injured.

Assuming the tribuni was even alive, of course. That wasn't a foregone conclusion, by any means.

Though it would have gutted him to do so, I was confident Caius would have told me the same thing. The mission was the mission, and it had gone surprisingly smoothly, given the unexpected appearance of a hostile army on our tails.

The next stage of the plan was a little bit murkier. I didn't dare take Kaeto to either Utrea or Eburos. That would be the spark that ignited the war we were all trying to avoid. We had to get out of the skies as fast as possible, though.

I need someplace remote enough that no one will stumble across us, but still well inside Alyrion territory, I told Xael. *Preferably with potable water and foraging, since I'm not sure how long we'll be there.*

I received the dragon equivalent of a thoughtful grunt in reply, and Xael veered right, his wing dipping as he banked through the air.

Kaeto was still rigid beneath my looped arm, his breathing coming fast and ragged. I really hoped he didn't try to do anything stupid before we reached wherever we were going.

Thankfully, he didn't. Xael eventually descended into a sheltered valley, located some distance west along the same mountain range we'd been traversing. The area appeared largely arid, but a strip of green meandered along its center, signaling the presence of a waterway large enough to support vegetation.

Foraging might be a challenge, but there would at least be some game nearby. Xael could hunt meat for us if it came to that.

The dragon swooped in for a landing on a flat patch of ground not far from the stream. I braced for the familiar double-thump as his hind legs hit the ground, followed by his front legs. I was off Xael's back before Kaeto finished righting himself from where he'd nearly impaled his own chest on the sharp spine he'd been using as a handhold.

I backed off a few steps and pulled the stolen knife from my belt again, watching impassively as Xael gave a full-body shake. Kaeto yelped and went tumbling off his perch, but he rolled as he landed and came up with surprising speed, pulling a dagger from his boot as he did.

His gaze seesawed back and forth between Xael and me. He held the dagger outstretched, but its point wavered between his two targets.

"Yeah… you'll want to rethink that approach, *sire*," I said. "A dagger's not much use against a dragon. And if you somehow manage to take me out when you can barely stand up, he'll be *irritated*. You wouldn't like him when he's irritated."

That part was a bluff. If Kaeto *did* somehow manage to get a blade through my heart, Xael would be too busy dying to be irritated about it.

I could see Kaeto weighing his chances… see the moment he realized just how badly the odds were stacked against him. He straightened, favoring his left knee, and deliberately put the dagger back in his boot.

"Perhaps you'd care to explain yourself, Darra Firebrand," he said, with admirable steadiness. "Somehow I have a hard time believing the idyllic hamlet of Sydrilla has been secretly raising dragons within the empire's borders."

"Funny you should say that," I told him, fingering the edge of my own blade with clear intent. "In fact, it's the subject of dragons inside the empire that I'd like to discuss with you, *Your Majesty*."

NINE

I might have imagined the look of confusion that flashed behind Kaeto's eyes, so quickly was it gone. In less than a second, it was replaced by the all-too-familiar smooth mask that was the emperor's normal public face.

"I daresay you're far more of an expert on the subject than I," he said. "What are you—Eburosi? I *thought* there was something odd about your accent."

"My accent is excellent, thank you very much," I snapped back. "And in case you haven't noticed, I'm the one asking the questions."

"I hadn't, since you've yet to ask me one," he replied coolly. "Perhaps you'd care to remedy that."

Gods, the man was infuriating even at dagger point.

I donned my own mask of indifference, watching him carefully as I spoke. "You're hiding four dragon eggs stolen from an Eburosi weyr. I require their location."

Kaeto froze—the barest hesitation.

"*You* require it, or your government does?" His eyes narrowed. "And that still wasn't a question."

This was the place where things got tricky. The moment I'd decided on this course of action, I'd

68

forfeited any direct connection with the Eburosi Tribal Council. If they were smart, they'd disavow all knowledge of me—along with any connection to the abduction of the Alyrion emperor. I fully intended to ensure they never had to make that decision, though.

"No government," I lied. "I represent... shall we say... *private interests*. There are other groups that want dragons, and you have four that aren't being guarded by either Utrea or Eburos. Trust me when I say, Eburos is *painfully* aware that those eggs are gone—and they have a good idea who took them. I just happened to be a bit faster off the mark than they were."

Kaeto's body was so still he might have been carved from rock. "Would it not be simpler to breed your own?" His gaze flickered to Xael before returning to me.

"Sure," I told him. "As soon as we acquire females. It's not like Xael's going to be laying any eggs. He doesn't really have the plumbing for it."

The dragon's mental huff was sour. Breeding was a bit of a sore point for both of us. There were few enough dragons in the world that we couldn't afford to waste a healthy male of breeding age. But Xael had never shown interest in mating with any of the available females.

That's because they're not very interesting.

I sent him a quelling thought in return. *I'll tell Rensa you said so, shall I?*

Not that Valeph's little white female dragon had eyes for anyone except her bronze companion, Panosh. That was a whole *other* issue.

"I see," said Kaeto, with the air of someone who was playing for time. That was fine. Now that I had him safely away from his phalanx of protectors, I had all the time in the world. He glanced at Xael again. "May I ask how you acquired this rather impressive specimen? Since, as you say, dragons and dragon eggs tend to be closely guarded."

"Found him in a cave," I said with a thin smile. "The old king of Utrea wasn't as successful at eradicating dragons in the wild as people seem to think."

Neither statement was untrue, technically speaking. I'd been a young girl when I accompanied my father and grandparents up to a cave in the foothills of northern Eburos, to see the first clutch of dragons ever hatched on the island. The eggs had come from the five original dragons rescued by the Utrean royal family. Xael had been among them—the first one hatched. I'd fed him tiny bites of rabbit meat from a pair of greenwood tongs, and fallen immediately and deeply in his thrall at the wise old age of eleven.

As for wild dragons, there were a handful still roaming the northern slopes of the Utrean mountains. Occasionally, people tried to tame them. Sometimes, they even survived the attempt.

"Did you indeed," Kaeto replied without inflection. "And then you somehow bonded with this wild dragon, before embarking on a quest to acquire more of the creatures for your mysterious *private interests*. How fascinating."

"Guess he recognized a kindred spirit," I said lightly. "*Firebrand*, and all that. However, as we've already established—I'm more interested in you answering my question about the stolen eggs. Preferably before my companion here gets impatient and decides you look like lunch."

Xael took the hint and puffed out a threatening cloud of smoky vapor, shaking his large head restlessly. Kaeto took a half step backward before he could catch himself, and I derived more satisfaction from that tiny lapse of self-control than I probably should have.

It was a bit of an open question what I'd do if Kaeto laughed in my face and told me to go to perdition. Killing him risked the resulting power vacuum being filled by someone even worse— someone who would still have access to dragons if Alyrios was able to hatch the eggs successfully. Leaving him alive had its own set of risks, especially if he decided I was lying through my teeth about being unaffiliated with Eburos.

My current plan was to shrug and fly away, leaving him alone in a remote valley with no weapons or shelter, and limited options for food. Xael could keep an eye on him for a day or two and see if hunger and exposure to the elements softened him up.

Kaeto wasn't his father. The old emperor, Constanzus, had been a warrior of renown— traveling at the head of his expansive army during the period of Alyrion conquest and expansion in the decades before I'd been born. Kaeto might be a deft hand with a sword thanks to Aelio's patient training, but he hadn't spent his adult life campaigning in rough conditions.

He was, at his heart, a palace brat. I was willing to bet he'd have no idea what to do with himself in a place such as this.

Perhaps he was aware of the risk that I'd simply fly off and abandon him, because his gaze on me was calculating. I let him stew, knowing he didn't exactly have a wide array of options before him.

"Very well," he said, once the silence became stifling. "I wish to propose an exchange, in that case. I have information you desire, and you have a capability I presently lack."

"Or," I countered, "hear me out on this one. You could tell me what I want to know, and I won't order Xael to kill you. Maybe I didn't make it clear earlier—but this isn't a negotiation."

"*You* hear *me* out, firebrand," he said, as unruffled as though I hadn't just threatened his life. "I will give you the location of your four dragon eggs, along with some additional information that I suspect you will find both interesting and useful."

This was Kaeto, so it obviously wasn't going to be that straightforward.

"But?" I prompted.

"But first," he went on, "I require your assistance in locating and freeing Tribuni Aelio from the raiders."

My thoughts stuttered to a halt, because that wasn't a request I'd anticipated. Xael perked up in interest.

"What makes you think he's still alive?" I asked.

Tension stiffened Kaeto's shoulders and neck, making the tendons in his jaw stand out. "It takes a fair amount of effort to extract a fallen rider who's been pinned under his mount. It takes considerably less effort to check for a pulse. If he'd been dead, I doubt they'd have bothered pulling him free."

"That doesn't mean they didn't kill him afterward," I pointed out, sparing another thought for my mentor Caius' old friend. "Especially if he didn't tell them what they wanted to know." I raised an eyebrow—a small reminder that Kaeto was currently embroiled in a similar predicament.

"Perhaps," Kaeto said. "But for a group seemingly bent on attacking the imperial retinue, the palace tribuni would have far more value as a hostage than as a corpse."

"You think the raiders knew who they were attacking," I said.

Kaeto's expression soured. "The massive banners flying at the front of the imperial retinue tend to be a bit of a giveaway. In general, they act as a deterrent. But in this case..."

"Not so much," I finished for him.

Deresta's flaming tits. I was actually considering his proposal, wasn't I?

Of course you are, Xael sent. His mental presence sounded tired but resigned.

Caius would skin me alive if he knew I'd agreed to this madness. He'd also do the exact same thing I was contemplating if he were here in my place—the noble old bastard.

"All right," I said with a sigh, gesturing at a nearby flat boulder jutting out of the ground. "Have a seat. Let's figure out what a plan to raid the raiders might look like."

TEN

Unfortunately, the same logistical issues that had prevented me from trying to rescue Aelio during the battle in the canyon still held true.

If he'd been pinned under his horse, he was most likely injured. That would make transporting him to safety much more difficult. If I took Kaeto along, and he somehow got access to a horse stolen from the bandits, I had little doubt he'd try to make a run for it, loyalty to Aelio or no. I doubted Xael could carry all three of us, especially if Aelio had a broken leg or something.

As if that wasn't enough, the longer we waited, the colder the trail would be.

This was a stupid plan from start to finish, and I was a stupid woman for considering it in the first place. I leaned back on the boulder I was using as a seat and contemplated my imperial captive.

"So… I can't trust you not to attempt escape," I told him. "And I can't afford to waste time. If we leave it too long, following the bandits' trail will become next to impossible, even from the air. Tell me—what would you do if you were in my position?"

Kaeto poked at the rabbit carcass roasting on a rough wooden spit with distaste. "Hmm. A difficult conundrum, I agree."

The emperor of Alyrios had adjusted to his situation as my captive with more grace than I might have given him credit for.

Perhaps I shouldn't have underestimated him. I knew from Caius' stories that Kaeto's older brother had made a spirited attempt to have him assassinated when he'd found out Kaeto had ambitions of taking the throne. Kaeto had spent time injured and on the run before. He'd also spent time as a captive.

The erstwhile emperor gave the rabbit a final disgusted prod. To be fair, it probably *was* overcooked at this point—which was better than risking parasites from leaving it undercooked. He sat back and flexed his swollen left knee.

"I suppose I'd leave me here," he said slowly. "No one knows where I am, and it's not as though I'm going to hike back to civilization on this leg. Assuming I knew in which direction civilization lay… which, obviously, I don't."

Hmm. It wasn't a terrible idea, now that I thought about it. Maybe that labyrinthine brain of his was good for something after all.

"And what about transporting Aelio?" I asked. "If he's badly injured, he won't be able to travel by dragonback."

Kaeto's expression soured as he leveled a glare at Xael. "I certainly wouldn't wish that infernal beast's flailing on anyone with a broken leg or a shattered pelvis." He paused for a moment. "Not unless they'd crossed me first, at least."

"And Aelio has never crossed you, I gather?"

Kaeto snorted. "If so, he's been impressively circumspect about it." He paused, growing thoughtful. "The force that descended on us in the canyon was a large one. And they were some considerable distance away from the nearest source of supplies."

"*Wagons*," I realized. "They must have wagons to carry provisions. Not in the mountains, though—the terrain is too rough."

"But wherever they've set up their base camp," Kaeto finished.

If Aelio was too badly injured to ride, I could transport him—and any other surviving prisoners—to the nearest town in a wagon liberated from the attacking force. It wasn't a perfect plan. A wagon in hostile territory was vulnerable without guards. I would only have *one* guard... but it would be a guard of the flying and fire-breathing variety.

Xael could follow us at a high enough altitude not to draw undue attention from the ground. In the event of an attack, he could be there in moments to defend us. My dragon looked up from the unidentifiable charred animal he was devouring and offered the mental equivalent of a shrug—as if to say, *sure, no big deal*.

"This could work," I said aloud. "I mean, assuming Aelio is alive, and not languishing at death's door. There are no guarantees."

"You do surprise me," Kaeto said tartly. He abandoned the cooking rabbit and lounged back on his makeshift seat as though it was a throne. "Bring me back a personal item of his, and I will answer your questions. Unless, of course, a bear or a lion appears to devour me in your absence."

"Surely you can fashion a spear from a branch and defeat the lion in single combat," I told him, with precisely no sympathy whatsoever. "You are the *emperor*, after all. Maybe the bards will write a song about the epic battle one day."

I tried not to notice how well dishevelment suited him. Ever since that first evening when he'd come in with Aelio, sweat-soaked and bruised after sparring, I'd had more aesthetic appreciation for *mussed-up Kaeto* than for *buttoned-up Kaeto*.

"You are a disrespectful hellcat who'd be flogged in the public square, were we back at my palace," he said.

"And you're not very civil for someone whose continued survival depends on not pissing me off," I retorted, in a perfectly pleasant tone. "Be glad that Aelio was nice to me when he thought I was a serving girl. Otherwise, I wouldn't bother with this."

Kaeto spared me a thin, unpleasant smile. "A polite and agreeable demeanor is politically useful for a palace tribuni," he said. "Less so for an emperor."

"Evidently," I told him, and went to rescue the rabbit from the fire before it became completely inedible.

⤜👑⤛

Before dawn the following day, I left Kaeto armed with his collection of hidden daggers and provisioned with a few more rabbits, dressed and weighted at the edge of the rushing stream to keep them from spoiling.

I did my best to ignore the little voice that whispered to me, pointing out that this was one of the more hare-brained schemes I'd ever come up with—which was truly saying something. This time, the voice sounded an awful lot like Orlene. I wondered if she and the others had made it back over the border into Utrea yet.

Not yet, Xael conveyed.

I supposed he would know… at least, whether they'd reunited with their dragons. Even without a mating bond, dragons in close-knit combat groups seemed to have a sixth sense for their compatriots' emotional state. Xael would feel the excitement over his nestmates' reunion with their riders.

"All right. I'm leaving. Don't do anything I wouldn't do," I told Kaeto, as I stepped up onto Xael's extended wing and mounted. Once again, I wished for a saddle. The stupid split skirt I was wearing hadn't been designed to rub against dragon scales for hours at a stretch, and it wasn't as though I had access to any other clothing under the circumstances.

Kaeto offered me another of those thin, humorless smiles. "I have a feeling that your admonition offers a considerable degree of latitude."

I lifted a shoulder, unconcerned. "Try to avoid hurling lit oil lamps, at least," I counseled. "This brush is dry enough that a wildfire could be nasty."

Xael punctuated the words with a warning puff of smoke. Kaeto's jaw tightened as he waved it away from his face. I'd noticed that he no longer flinched whenever the dragon looked at him sideways, which was interesting.

"Good luck," he said, as though the words had been forced from him. "If only because I have no desire to starve to death on stringy rabbit meat if you get killed."

I placed a hand theatrically over my heart and bowed low over Xael's neck, as though deeply touched by his words. "Your Imperial Majesty honors me," I replied, in a tone of deep sarcasm. "I'll be back as soon as I can with news, one way or another."

With that, I urged Xael into flight, taking no satisfaction whatsoever at the way the downdraft from his massive wings sent Kaeto staggering.

The flight back to the area where the attack had taken place seemed to last twice as long as it had the first time. It gave me plenty of time to second guess every single decision I'd made over the course of the past few days.

On the positive side, the calm weather meant that the tracks left by the passage of dozens of horses hadn't been blown or washed away yet. As I'd suspected, the trail led south, rather than back to the north, toward Amarius. It made sense—they'd clearly intended to take prisoners. There was no benefit in dragging those prisoners through the larger melee that had been taking place at the rear of the retinue.

The site of the ugly, two-pronged battle was a mess. I hoped, with a little pang of guilt, that the plucky pony I'd been riding had successfully escaped the carnage. My quick and dirty body count from the air showed that there were roughly six dozen dead, and no one had cared enough to bury them. They lay where they had fallen.

The death toll seemed to be roughly equal between the two sides — the attackers had prevailed mostly thanks to weight of numbers, from the look of things. Aelio definitely didn't number among the abandoned corpses in the ravine — I'd made sure of that much before I committed to continuing the mission.

Kaeto's party had been nearly at the halfway point along the canyon trail when Xael arrived to extract us from the battle. The mass of horse tracks emerging from the far end of the ravine continued south along the same route we would have traversed toward Heleva. Only when the mountainous terrain gentled to foothills did Xael swerve off the beaten path, following the trail into the gently rolling landscape.

The bandits' camp lay in a verdant valley, and it had an air of semi-permanence to it. Tents vied for space with round, wood-framed structures stretched with hide walls and thatched with native grasses.

There were, in fact, several wagons parked in the flat, central area of the settlement.

More importantly, there were a handful of slumped figures tied to the wheels of those wagons — figures wearing the distinctive leather armor of the Imperial Guard. My heart lifted in relief.

"Bull's eye," I muttered, and swung Xael around for a final approach.

ELEVEN

With an unprepared force lacking appropriate dragon harpoons for defense, it should be simple enough to drive off everyone in the camp who wasn't tied to a wagon.

Try not to torch everything, I ordered Xael. *I want to raid their supplies before we leave.*

The dragon's mild disappointment flared through the bond. But he dutifully swooped down from above, letting loose with a piercing shriek that would have woken the dead—much less a few dozing guards.

Within moments, panic erupted below us—people running out of structures with weapons in hand, only to realize that swords and pikes weren't going to help them much against this enemy.

Can't I burn it just a little? Xael's mental voice sounded plaintive.

Maybe a few of the tents on the downwind side, I allowed, figuring that if nothing else, that would get the camp moving faster. *But for the gods' sake, please don't roast the horses. We'll need them.*

With another gleeful shriek, Xael banked sharply. I gripped with my knees, vowing to liberate a decent pair of trousers—preferably from someone with a small enough build that I wouldn't swim in them. Xael arched his neck, his ribcage swelling beneath me as he opened his jaws and breathed fire.

The alarm below turned to screams. Humans ran from the flames in one direction, while several horses broke their tethers and galloped off in the opposite direction. I sighed, ducking close to Xael's neck to avoid the blowback of heat and smoke. I had a feeling I was going to be trekking through the valley to catch a team of panicked draft horses for the getaway wagon before this mission was over.

No survivors except the captives, I ordered.

Mild surprise threaded through the bond. As well it might—I was always the one telling Xael *not* to cause mayhem.

It wasn't the first time we'd killed humans. It *would* be the first time we'd killed them on this large of a scale. I prodded cautiously at my own feelings, finding sick queasiness swirling together with military practicality.

These people had seen Xael. They'd seen Emperor Kaeto flying away on dragonback. There was no guarantee that a messenger hadn't ridden out to report to someone after the battle in the ravine. But it would still be a hell of a lot easier to keep the news of a dragon causing mayhem inside the borders of Alyrios contained if most of the eyewitnesses were dead.

Predictably, the panicking bandits fled from their tents and buildings to open ground. In the absence of useful cover—and very little cover was useful during a dragon attack—they died in a hail of flame from above.

I locked the echoes of agonized screaming in a little box, and then I locked the little box away in the dark space behind my ribs. The resulting grass fire crept toward the edges of the makeshift settlement, but the passage of feet and horses had trampled the area around the structures down to bare dirt. The wind was light enough that it probably wouldn't blow any sparks onto the thatched rooves.

I brought Xael in for a landing, far enough from the parked wagons to hopefully prevent any of the bound imperial captives from succumbing to a heart attack at our sudden nearness.

Cover me, I ordered, jogging forward to scoop up a sword that had fallen from the hand of its fleeing owner. The hilt was designed for a man's grip, but I had long fingers. If nothing else, it was definitely a step up from the stolen paring knife I'd used to kidnap Kaeto.

Any bandits who'd stayed quiet and hidden inside their tents were likely to be the smart ones. It still wasn't a great strategy during a dragon attack, but it at least showed a little bit more foresight and self-control than charging into an open field to die.

I twisted my wrist, gauging the balance of the blade. It was low quality… poorly made. But if you slashed it across a man's throat or stabbed it between his ribs, it would get the job done all the same.

Giving the layout of the settlement a quick once-over, I spared only the briefest glance at the bound captives by the wagons. There were three, and one of them was, indeed, Tribuni Aelio. I had the fleeting impression of ghastly pale skin and a leg that looked... *not quite right.*

Starting at the edge of the camp located farthest from the burning tents, I crept up to a doorway and flung back the flap—my sword held at the ready. After confirming it was empty, I moved to the next, and the next, and the next.

When I reached the more permanent looking structures near the center of the encampment, I found that the first two contained supplies. Burlap sacks of grain and flour lay stacked on wooden planks to keep them off the ground. Weapons hung from the walls. I resisted the urge to go knife-shopping before clearing the rest of the camp, but it would be nice to be properly armed when I left.

The third building held a similar cache of supplies. It also held two bandits, who shrieked deafening battle cries and lunged for me as I poked my head through the doorway.

I danced backward with a curse, not willing to clash in the confined space of the entryway. *"Bit of help here?"* I snapped, trying to call up the muscle memory for defending against multiple opponents.

A feint missed my shoulder by inches as I was busy blocking my other opponent's lunge. Despite the poor quality of their weapons, these weren't conscripted farmers or shopkeepers. These men had been soldiering long enough to know what it meant to fight for your life.

I ducked and spun to the side, a grunt of pain escaping me as a sword hilt grazed my temple—an attempted knock-out blow. It was enough to get the second attacker behind me, though.

In the normal course of things, purposely putting an opponent behind you was, shall we say, *not recommended*. When you had a dragon watching your back, however—

Crunch.

The scream of a man getting his spine crushed between sharp-toothed jaws cut off abruptly. The attacker who'd nearly taken my head off paused for a critical moment, gaping at his companion's grisly demise in horror. I wrenched the poorly balanced sword into position and stabbed it into his gut—an ugly, clumsy thrust that would have had Caius marching me straight back to the training yard for a week of drills.

Still... you couldn't argue with results. My opponent's weapon fell from suddenly nerveless fingers. He gagged, blood spilling from his mouth, and doubled over. I twisted the blade and wrenched it free as he crumpled slowly toward the ground. Kicking him over to sprawl on his back, I finished him off with a slash across the throat.

A look around reassured me that no one else was rushing out of hiding to attack me—a fact which might have been related to the presence of a massive dragon standing over the crushed body of one of their comrades.

My head rang like a bell after the blow I'd taken. Fortunately, my vision wasn't blurry, and I didn't feel dizzy, so it didn't seem like any serious damage had been done.

Hardest part of your body, Xael suggested.

Oh, my gods, Xael—fuck you and the egg you hatched from, I sent back.

I ignored the smoky snort of amusement that generated, in favor of grimly continuing my tent-to-tent search of the camp. When I failed to turn up any additional bandits, I moved to the three bedraggled and injured prisoners.

In addition to Aelio, there was a guard with his left arm tied up in a makeshift sling, and another with half his face swollen black and blue, who didn't really seem aware of his surroundings. You could tell because he was just sort of sitting there, staring into the middle distance, while the other two darted wide-eyed gazes between me, the dragon, and the flames crackling merrily around the edges of the camp.

Aelio's face was tight with pain and weakness, but he was the first to successfully unstick his tongue.

"*Darra*?" he rasped. "Is that you? Or do you perhaps have a twin sister I should know about? Because... I'm sorry to be so slow, but I am *extremely* confused right now."

TWELVE

"Hello, Aelio," I said airily, crouching down to examine him properly. "No twin sister, just me. Bit of a long story, and one we don't have time for right now. Short version—the emperor sent me after you. He's safe. Well, he's got a bruised knee after taking a tumble, but nothing compared to this." I jerked my chin at his right leg.

While the tribuni was still bound and couldn't make a fuss about it, I deftly liberated a beaten metal pin formed in the shape of an eagle from his jerkin. I'd noticed he regularly wore it back at the palace, so it should suffice as proof for Kaeto when I returned to him later. Aelio was still in shock, but he scowled at me as I casually pocketed it.

"Sorry—but I need a personal item to show the emperor," I told him with a thin smile. "Now, we're going to get you and the others safely to the nearest town, and I'm pretty sure that's Heleva. You can return to Amarius when you've recovered from your injuries. Is it just you three?"

In response to the question, Aelio's frowning expression turned bleak. I wouldn't have thought it possible for him to go any paler than he already was. I'd have been wrong in that assumption.

It was the guard with his arm in a sling who answered. "They took Vikas prisoner, too. But they killed him a few hours ago. Tortured him to death." His voice was rough with anger, and possibly grief as well.

"They thought to loosen my tongue." Aelio's words were soft. *Distant*. "By making me watch."

I covered a wince. Clearly, it hadn't worked.

"What did they want to know?" I asked, unable to stifle my curiosity. From the beginning, this entire attack had felt subtly *off*. These men had been more than simple bandits — that much was certain.

"They wanted details on the number of city guards and palace guards stationed in the capital," Aelio said, still in that deceptively mild voice that covered deeper emotions. "For that reason, I must insist that you return me directly to Amarius."

"Not happening," I told him. "You'll have to travel by wagon because of your injuries — and a wagon won't make it through that mountain pass we traversed. There's a garrison stationed at Heleva, isn't there? I'll make sure you arrive safely, and I can pass on your report to the emperor when I return to him."

Aelio's exhausted eyes moved past my shoulder, to the looming reptilian presence behind me.

"You have a *dragon*," he said, as though he hadn't quite felt ready to broach the subject before now.

"Yes," I replied. Xael arched his neck, preening.

"*How* do you have a dragon?" Aelio pressed, with admirable patience given the circumstances.

"Darra, you're a *serving girl*. Nothing about this situation makes the tiniest amount of sense!"

"Part of that long story I mentioned, I'm afraid," I said. "I'd advise you not to get too close to the dragon or try to hold eye contact, by the way."

The young guard with the injured arm jerked his wide-eyed gaze away from Xael abruptly. In reality, Xael was happy to hold a staring contest with anyone who cared to stare back at him—but making him out as dangerously unpredictable would hopefully keep Aelio from suggesting that I take him back to Amarius on dragonback.

I received the mental equivalent of an eyeroll, but Xael shook his head in clear threat and let out a billowing puff of smoke, playing his part as the dangerous beast. The two fully conscious prisoners gave satisfying flinches of fear in response.

"Where is His Imperial Majesty now?" Aelio demanded, as I reached forward to untie his bonds.

"On his way back to the palace," I lied. The knots had tightened into a solid mass, so I carefully sawed through the rope with the edge of the sword instead.

The tribuni's scowl deepened. "And the rest of our contingent?"

"Those that survived are with him. Those that didn't are still lying in the ravine where they fell." That was another lie, of course—and I'd happily keep feeding him untruths as often as necessary to keep him compliant.

Freed, Aelio flexed his hands and arms, rubbing at the sore muscles with swollen fingers. I moved to the other two guards and freed them as well. The man with the head injury continued to stare blankly at nothing, his arms falling to hang limp by his sides. The other one's arm had a nasty break below the elbow. A halfhearted attempt had been made to splint it—but it needed to be reset if it were to have a chance of healing properly. Unfortunately, that was going to have to wait until he got to Heleva.

"Is your leg broken?" I asked Aelio, eyeing the grotesquely swollen and twisted knee. His captors hadn't even bothered with a splint for the tribuni. Hell, they hadn't bothered to so much as slice his breeches open to look at the injury.

"Not sure," Aelio said through gritted teeth, prodding at it. "My horse landed on it."

He didn't ask if the handsome bay courser were still alive. He must have known already that it wasn't.

"Hmm," I said, freeing the paring knife from its hiding place in my belt. "Let's have a look, then."

The blade might have been fairly useless in a fight, but it was well suited to cutting open a trouser leg. Aelio hissed as the procedure tugged and pressed on the injury, but he didn't protest. For now, I cut the fabric around the top of his boot, knowing that if I tried to remove his footwear, it would be agonizing.

The leg was a mass of bruising, and the knee was swollen to grotesque proportions. Even so…

"That looks decidedly, uh, *wrong*," I said, battling an unexpected surge of nausea. "Sorry, Aelio, but I think it really is broken."

I tilted my head, trying to make sense of the odd bulge on the outside of the joint. The guard with the broken arm crouched across from me, grimacing in pain.

"Nah. That's a dislocated kneecap, is what that is. See?" He pointed to the odd divot at the front of Aelio's knee with his good hand.

Aelio gingerly pressed against the bulge, his pallid complexion taking on a greenish cast. "He's right, I think. Bloody *hell*."

Sure enough, the little bone that should have formed a knob at the front of the joint had been wrenched to one side beneath the force of the fall, or possibly the weight of the horse.

"You can usually push it back into place if you're careful," said the guard. "Probably would have been easier before the swelling got so bad, though."

"You've seen it done before?" I asked. "Can you talk me through it?"

I wasn't about to touch an arm with a compound fracture. I knew enough about injuries to be aware that I could easily leave the man's hand permanently paralyzed if I failed to set the bones correctly. But if there was a relatively simple procedure that could improve Aelio's odds of healing well, I was willing to try it.

The guard nodded. "My father was a physic. Sometimes I went with him on calls when I was young."

"Aelio?" I asked. "Are you game?"

Aelio gave a tight nod. "If it's possible, I'd prefer to have my kneecap back where it belongs, thank you very much."

I let out a slow breath. "Right. Better take your belt off, in that case."

As a soldier, Aelio knew exactly what I meant. While the guard explained the best way to push the kneecap into position, Aelio fumbled it off and doubled the thick leather, biting down on it.

With the guard leaning over my shoulder to offer commentary, I lifted Aelio's leg, bending the joint to a right angle. Supporting his calf with one hand, I tightened my jaw against a fresh surge of queasiness. Then I pressed the dislocated bone toward its correct position, while carefully straightening the leg at the same time.

Aelio groaned around the strap, the noise sharpening to a muffled cry as the patella popped back into place on the now-extended leg. Panting, he spat out the belt—his face gray-tinged and beads of sweat standing out on his forehead. His eyes rolled up, eyelids fluttering as he fought to hold on to consciousness.

"It'll need to stay splinted, so it doesn't slip out of place again," said the guard, who looked none too steady on his own feet.

I nodded. "I'll find some lengths of wood. We can use your belts to hold it in place." I indicated the third man, who now slumped against the wagon with his eyes closed. "What about him? Do you know anything we can do for his head?"

The guard looked abruptly exhausted. "If we had some ice, then maybe. But we don't. He's been in and out of things since the battle. Mostly out."

"We'll get him to some better help." Aelio's voice was reedy with pain.

I slipped away to scavenge some boards from one of the semipermanent structures, grabbing a couple of promising daggers and a scabbard for my stolen sword while I was at it. When Aelio's leg was splinted straight with the soldiers' belts strapping everything in place, my focus turned to getting a wagon ready for travel.

The fires had thankfully burned themselves out in the absence of a breeze. As expected, I had to go trekking out into the valley to retrieve two horses, along with a third to tie to the back of the wagon as a spare.

I should stick you in the harness instead, I grumbled silently to Xael.

The dragon scoffed, stretching his wings languidly. *I'd like to see you try, two-legs.*

I chose the wagon that seemed to be in the best condition and loaded it up with provisions, along with a pile of blankets and empty sacks to cushion the third guard's ride. Separately, I made up two sacks of supplies that might be useful for someone stuck in a valley with a sarcastic twat of an emperor. Tying the tops of the bags together, I slung them over Xael's shoulders, hooking them over a convenient spine.

To my immense irritation, the smallest trousers I could find to replace my ridiculous split skirt were still much too large. I rolled up the cuffs and tied a length of twine around the waist to keep them from sliding down.

After the shock of having his kneecap shoved into place started to wear off, Aelio began to rally. He and the conscious guard both ate and drank something, managing to get a bit of watered wine and a few bites of bread into the man with the head injury.

As I was hauling the third man into the back of the wagon in preparation for departure, I could feel Aelio's eyes on me like a physical weight. I ignored the feeling as best I could—but that only worked until he grasped my arm as I walked by him, bringing me to a halt.

He was using the side of the wagon as a brace to remain upright, and it wouldn't have taken much for me to free myself and send him tumbling. I held very still, waiting to see what this was about... but my nerves thrummed a warning.

Aelio hadn't risen to his station as palace tribuni through luck alone. He was a formidable soldier, and a formidable strategist.

"You're lying to us," he said, quietly enough not to carry to the guard with the broken arm, who was working one-handed to help organize the supplies. "About a number of different things, I suspect."

I met his stormy blue eyes and held them. "Withholding information isn't the same as lying," I told him—though of course I was lying about that as well. "Consider the possibility that you don't know *every single thing* about what's going on behind the scenes at the palace. You said it yourself—this wasn't a simple bandit attack."

A furrow of frustration formed between his brows in response to my stonewalling and misdirection.

"More importantly," I went on, "your choices right now are basically to stay here and die... or accept my help and get your men to safety. I'd suggest you focus on the details of the report you want me to pass on to the emperor. We leave at midday."

THIRTEEN

I had Aelio over a barrel, and he knew it. I suspected that was the only reason he hadn't kicked up more of a fuss as I herded him and the other guard into the wagon.

Well... that and the dragon watching over things with beady, unamused eyes the same color as polished tanzanite.

I'd been concerned that I'd have to drive the wagon myself, but Aelio stiffly informed me that his hands weren't the issue, only his leg. With one man who couldn't walk without help, another who only had one working arm, and a third who appeared to be more vegetable than human at this point, it wasn't going to be a pleasant journey for anyone involved.

Fortunately, by my estimate, we were less than a day out from Heleva by cart. If the men got into trouble along the way, I could swoop down from the sky in moments to help them. That would have to be good enough, because the prospect of riding in the wagon and dodging Aelio's pointed questions for the entire journey was not an enticing one.

The draft horses snorted, their eyes rolling behind the leather blinders as they tried to keep tabs on Xael. I'd released the remaining riding horses who hadn't already broken their tethers, letting them all run free. With access to grass and water, they'd be all right until some enterprising group from Heleva came and rounded them up to sell.

In addition to a couple of bags of provisions scavenged from the storage structures and slung over Xael's scaly shoulders, I'd also added some rolls of canvas to use for blankets and a tent back in the valley where I'd left Kaeto. That way, if His Imperial Twatness was stubborn about handing over the location of the dragon eggs, I'd at least have shelter and something to sleep on.

Lastly, I'd liberated a small but useful arsenal of weapons for myself and the others. All in all, I was feeling better about things than I had been a day ago.

"The main road lies in that direction," I told Aelio, pointing east. "You'll make Heleva if you drive all day and into the night. There should be enough of a moon for it. Or you can sleep in the wagon overnight and finish the journey in the morning, but that increases the chance you'll run into more bandits."

It was a lot to ask of people with serious injuries. I had a feeling that it *wasn't* a lot to ask of Aelio. I could almost guarantee he'd drive all night long without complaint, if doing so meant getting his men to safety faster.

The tribuni's pale eyes burned into mine. "You will pass on my report about the attackers to His Majesty the moment you return to him."

"I'll make sure he gets it," I said. And, hey, that part was even the truth—probably. A hint of potential armed insurrection against the imperial throne might make a useful lever when it came to prying information out of the stubborn sod. If nothing else, the sense of added urgency could be helpful.

Aelio tilted his head, examining me. "You saved his life once before, Darra. Twice, if you're telling the truth about getting him away from the bandits. But you should know—if I discover you've caused any harm to come to him, you'll have made a deadly enemy."

The threat wasn't unexpected.

"I don't want to make an enemy of you, Aelio," I told him. "Even if I don't see what Kaeto could possibly have done to gain such loyalty from you. You know better than anyone what he's like."

Even as the words left my lips, I knew I shouldn't have said them aloud. *Crap*. That accusation had come out before I'd fully thought it through.

Aelio saw immediately that it had been a slip. He could have pounced on it... taken it as proof that I wasn't working on Kaeto's side.

"Yes," was all he said. "I know exactly who he used to be, and I also know who he is now. More importantly, I know how close Alyrios came to languishing under the rule of a *true* monster."

I drew breath to say something else, then thought better of it. I'd already made one mistake because I felt like I knew Aelio personally through the stories Caius had told me about him. But Aelio wasn't a story. He was a loyal servant of the emperor—and in this context, that made him my enemy.

"I'll be watching over you from above," I said shortly, and crossed to mount Xael.

⚬⟡⚬

I waited until the wagon was safely away before allowing Xael to burn the remains of the settlement to the ground. There was no way to know when, or even if, someone would stumble across the carnage of bodies consumed by flame.

The idea that the entire camp had mysteriously caught fire, and the bandits hadn't been able to outrun the destruction, was questionable at best. Even so, it didn't quite scream *dragon attack* to the same degree as finding them dead in a circle of burned grass, while most of the nearby structures remained untouched.

Happily, the weather stayed calm enough that the new fire didn't spread far. When I was confident it wouldn't rage out of control, I directed Xael to fly after Aelio and his men. It took no time at all to catch up to the plodding wagon on the main road. We described lazy circles high above to keep pace with it.

The vehicle and horses were little more than small brown dots far below, but it would be obvious enough if they stopped—or if others approached them. More importantly, at this range, anyone on the ground would have to really be looking before they noticed us wheeling distantly in the blue sky. That's what I was counting on, anyway.

So many people spent their whole lives staring down at the dirt beneath their feet, rather than up at the clouds.

The next several hours were deathly boring, but at least this time I had access to food and water.

Must be nice for some, Xael grumbled.

Confident that my faithful dragon wasn't truly on the verge of starvation, I made sympathetic noises and snuck another piece of flatbread out of the provision bag. Below us, traffic on the road had grown more commonplace as the wagon descended from the foothills to the flatlands. That traffic decreased as the sun went down—few people wanted to ride or drive in the dark if they didn't have to.

Only when the flickering torches atop the walls of Heleva came into view did I finally peel away and head north again. The city's garrison would accept Aelio and his soldiers into their fold. I rubbed a finger over the metal eagle pin hooked to my makeshift belt for safekeeping. My duty to Caius' friend had been discharged. Whether it also ended up being the key to Kaeto's secrets remained to be seen.

⁓ ♛ ⁓

The emperor of Alyrios had at least been able to keep a campfire going in my absence. It was good to see that the nobility was capable of snapping scrub branches into pieces and occasionally tossing one into the flames as needed. I wondered idly how he'd fared with the rabbit carcasses.

If he didn't eat them, I will, Xael complained, gliding in for a landing with admirable silence— mostly so he could enjoy Kaeto's yelped curse and inelegant scramble when we appeared out of nowhere at the edge of the circle of firelight with a heavy double-thump of landing.

"Sorry, did we startle you?" I asked in my best tone of innocence, sliding down from Xael's back. My legs and hips felt rusted solid after so much time in the air, and I desperately needed a piss. First things first, though.

Kaeto staggered to his feet as I closed the distance between us. His knee seemed a bit better. I tossed Aelio's glinting pin at his chest. He flinched and fumbled it, nearly dropping it and then hissing as the sharp point pricked him.

I raised an eyebrow.

"One rescue, successfully completed," I told him. "Aelio's alive. Dislocated kneecap and some other miscellaneous bumps and bruises, but he and the other two surviving soldiers will be safe inside Heleva's walls by now."

Kaeto's wary gaze flicked from me to the pin in his hand. He'd donned his unreadable mask as I spoke.

"How terribly efficient of you, firebrand," he said, his tone giving nothing away. "Of course, I have only your word that you didn't pluck this bauble from his rotting corpse—and we both know what an accomplished liar you are."

"Yes, we do," I agreed. "So, I suppose you'll have to decide whether or not to believe me when I pass on his report about his time in the so-called bandits' captivity."

His brows twitched together. Maybe it was just the firelight, and the scare Xael had given him, but the dark smears under his eyes and the pale cast of his skin spoke to a distinct lack of sleep.

"What report?" he demanded, his tone growing sharp.

I smiled sweetly at him. "Turns out, your would-be assassins are *extremely* interested in details of the defenses in Amarius. Number of troops, palace guard versus city guard, shift changes, that sort of thing. Sorry to be the bearer of bad news, *sire*... but apparently, you've got someone sniffing around your throne—and it seems they aren't playing around."

FOURTEEN

The fire behind Kaeto's gray eyes, which had been banked to embers since his capture, flared to violent life. I felt the shift like a jolt to the chest.

"Take me back to Amarius." The words were ice. "*Now.*"

"Tell me where you're hiding the dragon eggs, and I'll consider it," I retorted.

Kaeto's fixed stare felt like standing under a tree in the seconds before lightning struck. He twitched toward me, as though he might attack.

I stood my ground, aware of Xael's head snapping up behind me in response to the hint of aggression. Kaeto froze—not yet moved to suicidal behavior, apparently. I could see the seething frustration behind his stony expression... his absolute fury at his own impotence.

"Well?" I prompted.

Xael's sudden distraction tore my focus away from the tense standoff at what felt like the worst possible moment.

What is it? I asked.

The others are here. Excitement and pleasure flooded the bond.

"What?" I yelped, unable to smother the word.

The others could only mean one thing in this context. In disbelief, I craned to look up at the night sky.

"You will at least give me the courtesy of your attention when you're threatening me with a bloody dragon!" Kaeto snarled.

A sudden downdraft sent him stumbling back a step, the disturbance announcing the arrival of two more *bloody dragons*. Heavy wings cut through the air; Rensa and Panosh coming in for a landing on either side of Xael.

Kaeto gaped at them. "What the *hell*, firebrand!" he snapped, his voice like a whip.

Orlene and Valeph slid smoothly down from their mounts, entering the circle of firelight.

"What the *hell*, you two!" I demanded, unconsciously echoing my captive. "You're supposed to be—"

I cut myself off, aware that I couldn't exactly shout *'You're supposed to be on your way to Eburos!'* in front of Kaeto.

"—not here!" I finished lamely.

"Friends of yours, I take it?" Kaeto said through gritted teeth. "Oh, good. My evening is complete."

"Er… who is this person?" Valeph asked cautiously, eyeing the disheveled emperor with clear misgivings.

"You may address me as *Your Imperial Majesty*," Kaeto said coldly.

Silence fell, broken only by the crackle of the campfire.

"Darra…" Orlene said slowly. "Please tell me I'm misreading this, and you haven't kidnapped the emperor of Alyrios without telling us first."

My jaw worked, my teeth grinding together unpleasantly. "I prefer to think of it as having rescued the emperor of Alyrios from an organized attack of bandits, which may well be connected to an attempted coup in the capital."

"An interesting interpretation of events." Kaeto's tone could have dissolved varnish from wood.

"And to express his gratitude, His Imperial Majesty was just about to tell me where the stolen dragon eggs are hidden," I went on, as though he hadn't spoken.

That got the others' attention.

"Was he, indeed?" Valeph murmured. "How terribly forthcoming of him."

The magician's disconcerting pale eyes fell on Kaeto, glinting in the firelight. Orlene still looked like she wanted to drag me out of Kaeto's earshot and tear metaphorical strips from my hide—but at that, she, too, turned her glare on my captive.

For his part, Kaeto appeared to be calculating fresh odds like a seasoned gambler at the gaming tables.

"Ah. Yes," he said. "The eggs. As you have surmised, I have them in safekeeping—hidden deep in the catacombs that run beneath the imperial quarter in Amarius. You will not be able to reach their hiding place. The tunnel entrances are too small for your dragons to breach, and the eggs are too well guarded for you to fight your way to them on foot."

My stomach sank.

Kaeto lifted his chin. "Return me to the palace, and I will take you to them. If my throne is at risk, perhaps we can come to a mutually beneficial arrangement."

"He's lying," Val said.

I frowned. "Which part?"

Val tilted his head, birdlike. His gaze never left the emperor. "All of it, interestingly enough."

My attention jerked back to the emperor. Unease had crept behind Kaeto's mask.

"*Is* he, now?" I narrowed my eyes at him. "Better try again, *sire*."

He glared at me. "You take the word of this peasant freak over mine?"

Orlene snorted. "Well, yeah. We kind of do, actually."

I gave Kaeto the feral smile I'd inherited from my lion-shifter father. "Interesting fact—our esteemed associate possesses magic. Specifically, the ability to know instantly whether someone is telling the truth or not. Also—and I do mean this with the utmost respect, *Majesty*—you're a venomous serpent, and I wouldn't trust your word as far as I could throw you one-handed."

Kaeto jerked back as though he'd been slapped. "Pagan nonsense! Such superstition is nothing but the imaginings of the mentally deficient."

"Uh-huh," I said, nodding. "Sure. Tell him what you had for your last meal."

A hint of uncertainty flashed behind Kaeto's anger. "Fish."

"Lie," Valeph said, sounding bored.

"Berries," Kaeto said.

"Lie."

"Overcooked rabbit."

"Truth." Val raised an eyebrow.

"How did you and I meet?" I asked Kaeto.

"You threw a lit oil lamp at an assassin," he said.

"Truth." Valeph glanced at me. "An oil lamp? Seriously, Darra? I mean... *seriously?*"

I glowered. "What? It *worked*, didn't it?"

"Gods give me strength," said Orlene. "Right... what was the name of your first horse?"

Kaeto's lips were drawn back over his teeth. He was breathing heavily. "Nightmare."

Valeph sighed. "Lie."

"Storm."

"Lie."

"Basilisk."

"Lie."

A heavy pause.

"Peony." The word sounded like it had been pulled from Kaeto's lips by force.

"Truth."

"Aw," said Orlene. "That's actually adorable."

Kaeto was pale as a ghost in the flickering firelight—a man surrounded by enemies, whose only remaining weapon had been taken from him.

"How is this possible?" he rasped.

I couldn't hold back an irritated grunt. I might've lost my own magical heritage as a side effect of my dragon bond with Xael, but Kaeto's willful expression of ignorance still rankled like a burr under the saddle blanket.

"You brokered peace between the Deimonists and the pagans of Amarius. Don't pretend you've never seen magic before, Kaeto. If you do, Valeph will just tell us you're lying."

If anything, Kaeto went even paler.

"So, let's try this again," I said, with as much patience as I could muster. "*Where... are... the bloody... dragon eggs?*"

For a moment, Kaeto's mouth opened and closed like one of those fish he hadn't eaten for dinner. Then he swallowed, straightening his spine and squaring his shoulders.

"I have no idea what the hell you're even talking about," he said.

I growled at him in frustration. "Right, I *swear to the gods* I'm going to let one of these dragons tear your arms off. *Slowly.*"

"He's telling the truth," Val said quietly.

I whirled on him. "He's... *what?*"

"He's telling you the literal truth," Val repeated. "He doesn't know."

"Of *course* I'm telling the truth! I have no idea where these thrice-damned dragon eggs of yours are," Kaeto said tightly, beads of sweat shining on his brow. "Since *I'm not the one who ordered them stolen.* So, if you could please take me back to the *fucking* palace now, maybe I can stop whoever's plotting against the empire before they succeed in *taking my fucking throne.*"

FIFTEEN

This was a serious wrinkle, to put it mildly. Everything we'd done had hinged on Kaeto being behind the dragon eggs' theft.

"You're *sure* he's not lying?" I demanded, aware that my voice had gained an unpleasant, faintly hysterical note.

"Not a single word," Val said, peering at Kaeto like he was some kind of clever puzzle box before returning his attention to me. "Out of curiosity, how long has he been stringing you along?"

I thought back to the dangerous retrieval mission I'd undertaken in exchange for Kaeto's promise of the truth. He'd bluffed me without holding a single card in his hand.

Son of a bitch.

And yet, I couldn't fully regret the rescue—not when it meant Aelio's life had been spared.

"Long enough," I growled.

If Kaeto wasn't our target, we were back to square one. Worse than that, even. We had no clues whatsoever—the eggs could be anywhere on the continent. Anywhere in the *world*.

"So, now what the fuck do we do?" Orlene said, neatly echoing my own thoughts.

"Might I suggest," said the emperor, in the tone of someone reining in his temper with great difficulty, "that it would be a startling coincidence if the theft of multiple dragon eggs from Eburos, and someone attempting to take over the throne of Alyrios were unconnected?"

All three of us turned to look at him.

"You think," I said slowly, "whoever organized that raid on the imperial retinue also has the eggs?"

"That's quite a logical leap." Valeph was frowning, but he sounded uncertain.

"Is it, though?" Kaeto shot back. "Alyrios does not have *political coups*. Whoever is behind this must have a reason to think they can hold power, assuming they manage to grasp it in the first place."

"*You* staged a coup," I reminded him blandly. "You killed your own brother to keep him off the throne."

"I am an exception," Kaeto said haughtily, "to many things."

Orlene gave a derisive snort. "Clearly not an exception to the cliché that the nobility are full of themselves."

Val was still watching Kaeto curiously, however. "Interesting. And what course of action do you propose?"

"I propose, *freak*, that you take me back to the thrice-damned capital," Kaeto said. "Where, I might add, people don't require me to repeat myself *half a dozen bloody times*."

Abruptly, this oft-repeated demand to return to Amarius sounded... a lot less insane than it had before.

"I need to speak to one of my colleagues," I said. "Excuse us for a minute. Orlene, stay here and let Xael tear off the emperor's left arm if he tries anything."

Orlene's blue eyes conveyed that she had plenty to say to me herself. However, I suspected most of it would be delivered in an ear-splitting shout and liberally seasoned with cursing—which was why I jerked my head at Val to indicate he should follow me out of the circle of firelight instead.

"I'll make sure Xael cauterizes the stump while we're waiting for you to get back," Orlene said, her tone deceptively mild.

Val accompanied me silently through the sparse, scrubby vegetation, our way lit by starlight. With gritted teeth, I trekked far enough away from the rough camp that our words wouldn't carry back to Kaeto.

"Two questions." I began. "First, what in the hell are you and Orlene doing here? And second, where's Lavinio? My last note wasn't *that* vague about your orders."

Val was unruffled. "We arrived in Utrea to find Xael gone and the other dragons in a highly emotional state. Once we passed your message to your aunt, we sent Lavinio on to Eburos by ship. Then we flew back to see what you were doing that required Xael's help inside Alyrion territory—a question I'd still like answered, by the way. You mentioned something about raiders?"

I lifted a hand to rub at the corners of my gritty eyes. "I managed to gain a servant's position in the palace," I said.

"By throwing a lit oil lamp at an assassin," Val prompted, in that absolutely flat tone of his that somehow managed to sound even more judgmental than Orlene's yelling. "Thank you. I already know that part."

"Give me a break," I hissed. "Sometimes you have to work with whatever's to hand, all right?"

I dragged in a centering breath and let it out slowly.

"Anyway, the servant's position gave me the opportunity to accompany the imperial retinue on a diplomatic visit to Heleva. We'd just entered a narrow canyon when several dozen armed and trained fighters descended on us from the rear, driving us toward a second contingent blocking the ravine. I'd originally called Xael here to stage a kidnapping while Kaeto was away from the palace and therefore more vulnerable, but it turned into a rescue instead."

"Not a random attack of bandits, then," Val said grimly.

"No," I agreed. "As much as I hate to admit it, what Kaeto said back there makes a certain amount of sense. After the emperor escaped with me on dragonback, the raiders grabbed what prisoners they could, including the palace tribuni, Aelio. I agreed to find Aelio and free him in exchange for Kaeto giving me the location of the eggs."

My face burned at the reminder of how thoroughly I'd been played.

"And did you?" Val asked. "Free Aelio, I mean?"

"Yes. Xael burned the raiders' camp. I sent the tribuni and his two surviving soldiers on to Heleva in a stolen wagon. Apparently, their captors were extremely interested in details of the defenses inside the imperial quarter in Amarius."

Val nodded. "It sounds as though the emperor has reason to be concerned for his throne. So… what, if anything, do you intend for us to do about that?"

And that was the question, wasn't it?

"We can't exactly descend on the Alyrion capital with only three dragons," I said unhappily. "Amarius still maintains dragon harpoons for defense, for one thing."

"And it would instantly cause a war, for another." The words were dry. "We assumed from your last note that you wanted Utrea and Eburos to disavow you. How did you explain the fact that you have a dragon to Kaeto?"

"I told him I represented an unaffiliated faction that had managed to acquire dragons through covert means, and that we wanted more." I dug fingertips into my right temple, trying to root out the headache blossoming there. "We might still be able to run with that explanation, although I did tell him we had no female dragons and therefore couldn't breed our own. That might be an issue with Rensa here now."

"Will he be able to tell she's female?" Val asked.

"Maybe not." I steeled myself to accept the inevitable. "Look… I think we're going to have to play along with Kaeto and go back to the capital, simply because it's the only lead we've got."

"Without the dragons, you mean?" Val asked.

I nodded. "I know where we can get some horses that won't be missed. I left a couple dozen of the raiders' mounts milling around the valley where they were camped. We can fly there and round up four of them so we can ride back to Amarius."

"While leaving the dragons here in the mountains?" Val asked. "Or sending them back to Utrea?"

I thought about it for a moment. "Leaving them here. Every time they fly across the border, there's a chance someone will see them and assume King Rathanii is rattling his sword."

"Agreed," Val said. "Next question… do you think Kaeto will make a deal with us? One he'll stick to, I mean?"

Gods, would he?

"I think he's exceptionally motivated at the moment," I said. "I also think that the instant it's in his best interest to betray us, he'll throw us off the proverbial gangplank before you can say 'untrustworthy bastard.'"

"Wonderful," Val said. "I suppose we'll just need to make sure that the idea of betraying us doesn't become attractive."

With that, we returned to the others, to find Orlene and Kaeto still locked in a wary standoff.

"All right," I said. "We have a proposition for you."

"Do we?" Orlene asked skeptically.

"We do," I confirmed. "Kaeto, we'll get you back to Amarius, at which point you'll help us identify who was behind the raid on your retinue, and whether or not they have the stolen dragon eggs."

I was expecting some kind of counterproposal, so it was a surprise when Kaeto only crossed his arms and said, "Agreed. When do we leave?"

"In the morning," I said, recovering quickly. "We'll have to fly to the valley where the raiders were camped and steal some of their horses for the journey."

The emperor of Alyrios raised an eyebrow. "Why not fly directly to Amarius on dragonback? That would presumably be both faster and more impressive."

"Because Amarius has dragon harpoons, and I'd prefer not to be shot out of the sky the moment we're spotted," I said. "It's horses or nothing, *sire*."

Kaeto looked sour, but he nodded. "Very well." He ran a beady eye over the three of us. "I hope you're comfortable with fast riding, in that case. Because I won't be slowing down for you."

I matched his dark expression. "Don't worry. I think we all want answers as soon as humanly possible," I said.

SIXTEEN

The destroyed raider camp yielded not only horses, but more weapons as well—albeit, slightly singed. Orlene and I had a very calm and civil discussion about the merits of allowing Kaeto a sword, which I ultimately won by pointing out that he'd been armed with at least one dagger this whole time.

"Deresta's *tits*. You're an *idiot!*" Orlene said, very calmly and civilly. "Why are you in command, again?"

"Nepotism," Val replied sagely. "Pretty sure it's nepotism."

"It wasn't as though Kaeto was going to stab me with Xael standing around and waiting for an excuse to fry him," I said, doing my best to keep the defensive note out of my tone.

"And from now on, we won't have the dragons nearby to act as a deterrent." Orlene looked sour. "So why give him the means to stab you while he's standing even farther away?"

"Because we're not taking him to Amarius as our prisoner." I gave them both my best glare. "Because *he doesn't have the godsdamned dragon eggs,* and that means he was never our target in the first place."

"Oh, good. So, we're all friends now?" Val's tone was mild, which was almost but not quite enough to hide the underlying irony.

"We're four people whose aims currently run in parallel," I said evenly. "We'll take watch shifts at night in case you're worried he's going to stab us in our sleep. And if you're worried he's going to overpower all three of us while we're awake? Then I'm not sure what to tell you, except that maybe you chose the wrong line of work."

Orlene only scoffed, but at least that was the end of it.

The raiders' horses were a weedy bunch except for the draft animals, and skittish after their time running loose in the valley. The bay mare I ended up with was a step up from the pony I'd ridden out from Amarius, but Kaeto's captured gray gelding was definitely several steps down from his fine buckskin courser.

The other two ended up with a pair of rangy chestnuts, and after a short debate, we took two more nondescript geldings along as replacements, in case of lameness or colic.

Don't like this, Xael fretted inside my mind. *Horses are stupid.*

Getting skewered by a dragon harpoon while trying to infiltrate the capital of the Alyrion Empire is stupid, I retorted. *We'll call you and the others as soon as we can.*

Xael sent grudging acknowledgement, which was the best I was likely to get under the circumstances.

With the extra geldings carrying our meager collection of stolen supplies, we set off toward Amarius, riding hard. Kaeto had been grimly silent for the most part, not even hurling sarcastic barbs at us when it was obvious that we'd been discussing him behind his back.

The raiders' horses were tough; I had to give them that much. It had been three days' ride from the capital to the ravine where the imperial retinue had been attacked, and it would have taken us most of a fourth day to get from there to the burned-out camp on horseback rather than dragonback. The return journey to the city didn't involve pack mules or aging courtiers and was undertaken nearly twice as fast.

On the first day, we nearly made it to the town where the retinue had stayed on our second night of travel, only stopping to camp rough when we lost the moonlight. We were on the road again at the first hint of predawn.

"Keep up!" Kaeto snarled over his shoulder, kicking his mount into a fast canter.

I exchanged a glance with the others. Orlene and Val were grim-faced in the gray morning light, but they urged their horses to follow. I did the same, tugging on the lead of the pack horse I was ponying until it grudgingly kept pace.

We'd all seen Kaeto gritting his teeth as he limped stiffly around the camp in preparation for leaving. The first day of hard travel had done nothing to improve the state of his damaged knee, unsurprisingly. I couldn't help a twinge of respect for this soft palace brat, who nevertheless dragged himself into the saddle without complaint for another grueling day's ride.

That's because you like him, Xael said — unhelpful as always.

Like him? He's a lying, self-absorbed arsehole, I sent back.

There was a pause.

What's your point? Xael asked, with what seemed to be genuine confusion.

I pressed my lips together and pointedly turned my focus back to the road, where the figure of Kaeto crouched over his saddle some distance ahead. The second day passed much as the first had, except now we passed through towns clustered around the trade road.

We didn't stop in any of them, only slowing intermittently to a walk to let the horses blow when they grew too lathered. Aside from the bare minimum of pauses to let our mounts drink from streams and to relieve ourselves, we rode from dawn until dusk, and beyond.

I cringed internally to think what Carivel — one of my father's adoptive parents and the horse mistress of their village — would have to say about our hard use of the animals. But despite their coarse appearance, the raiders' horses were rugged and sturdy. None of them had yet to take a lame step.

We'd hobbled them and let them graze around the camp overnight, then rotated out the two spare pack animals with the ones Kaeto and Orlene — the heaviest riders — had been using on the first day. In return, they'd carried us all the way to Amarius in a shockingly short amount of time.

Ahead, the flickering torches and streetlamps winked in the distance like thousands of tiny fireflies. The city sprawled along the banks of the River Uvi, bounded on the far side by the ocean and surrounded on the other three sides by fertile farmland and grazing land.

We were losing what little moonlight there had been. The route this close to the capital was well-traveled during daylight, but largely deserted at this late hour. Travelers and honest tradespeople from the surrounding villages conducted their business when the sun was up. Only the desperate and the foolhardy stumbled around on an unlit road after dark.

Orlene urged her tired mount forward until she was riding abreast with Kaeto and me. "It's late. We should camp at the next crossroads and enter the city in the morning."

Kaeto made a noise of frustration. "Do you fear getting lost on the Great Southern Road, with Amarius shining like a beacon directly ahead of us? We will enter *tonight*."

He was only visible as a darker outline against the distant lights of the city. But even in silhouette, he hunched in the saddle like a much older man. Or like someone in pain from injuries worsened by lack of sleep and overexertion.

I tried to gauge the remaining distance. "It's… what? About two miles to the outskirts?"

Balancing those two miles of travel against the likelihood of Kaeto giving in without a fight, I made a decision. "Fuck it. Let's go. The sooner we can get inside the city walls, the safer we'll be… and the faster we can get some answers."

Orlene grumbled something but kept riding.

"I will have to get off and walk," Val said. "My horse is flagging."

Now it was Kaeto's turn to growl something under his breath—but he didn't spur his mount onward and leave us behind as I'd half expected him to.

Val dismounted, leading his mount and the second pack horse at a slow walk. We covered the final stretch of road that way, smallholdings springing up around us as we approached the city. The buildings grew larger and closer together, a gradual transition from rural to urban.

Parts of Amarius were walled, but the city had overflowed its bounds across the centuries. The southern trade road had guard posts, but no gate. As we passed by the two overlooking towers, no one emerged to stop us or question what we were doing abroad so late at night. No torches illuminated the structures.

"Shouldn't there be guards here?" Kaeto muttered.

A prickle of misgiving skittered along the back of my neck. "It's *your* trade road," I said. "Should there be?"

"I don't personally oversee every watchtower," Kaeto replied, waspish. "I employ other people for that."

As we entered the southern quarter with its thriving bars and taverns, we finally found signs of life. This part of Amarius never slept, but the late-night patrons appeared subdued compared to my previous visits.

"It does seem rather quiet tonight, does it not?" Val asked uneasily.

"Well," I mused, "I suppose the emperor of Alyrios *has* been missing for several days. Maybe the news has spread by now?"

We continued past the disreputable bar where I'd met in secret with Orlene, Val, and Lavinio; then past the slightly more reputable tavern where we'd left messages for each other. From there, crowded storefronts gave way to elegant marble buildings in the government district—empty and dark at this hour. Ahead loomed the high walls of the imperial quarter, the area lit brightly with torches.

All four of us had dismounted and were leading our horses by this point, Kaeto favoring his left knee heavily as he leaned on the saddle for support.

"At bloody *last*," he muttered, approaching the massive gate flanked by four armed and helmeted guards. His voice, gritty with travel and exhaustion, lifted in command. "You, there! Raise the gate!"

My prickle of disquiet from earlier hadn't lifted. Apparently, I wasn't the only one feeling it.

"Something's off," Orlene said, pitched for Val and my ears only.

One of the guards on the right lifted a hand. "Halt," he barked.

Kaeto stopped, more out of surprise than anything else, I thought. "*Excuse* me?"

"Bring that one forward," the guard told his nearest companion. "He matches the description of Kaeto—dark hair and sharp features. Check his right shoulder for a birthmark like a four-leaf clover."

My prickle of intuition exploded into alarm at the same moment Kaeto took a startled step backward and Orlene snarled, "*Blast!*"

SEVENTEEN

What are you doing?" Kaeto demanded, alarm and outrage battling for supremacy in his tone. "I am your *emperor*!"

The first guard grunted. "Right. Guess that simplifies things. Take him, men—the orders are dead or alive."

Kaeto, to his credit, was already going for his sword. So was I. Orlene was a heartbeat ahead of us, having already pulled hers free of its scabbard. Val, whose talents didn't lie with a longblade, skipped backward to get out of our way.

One of the guards who'd hung back bellowed for reinforcements, and my sinking stomach made an even deeper dive. Orlene, Val, and I might have managed to vault onto our exhausted horses and flee before we could be caught, but Kaeto could barely *walk* unaided.

A week ago, my mental calculations would have looked very different when it came to the injured emperor. When I'd believed him responsible for the theft of the dragon eggs, I'd needed him, it was true. But back then, there had been alternatives. Though the number might be small, other people had to know about the eggs as well.

If something had happened to Kaeto, I would've grumbled over my job being harder, but it wouldn't have been the end of the world.

Now, Kaeto was our best hope—mostly because the list of suspects had expanded to include pretty much everyone in Alyrios, and the eggs themselves could be absolutely anywhere. Having the empire's ruler nominally on our side might give us our only edge.

Plus, there was the small matter of the complete destabilization of the continent if he was successfully deposed and executed by whoever had taken control of the city.

Which is how I found myself fighting shoulder to shoulder with my people's hereditary enemy, guarding his weak left side as two soldiers made a spirited attempt to kill us. Right then, I *really* wished the quality of the raiders' weapons had been a bit better.

Even with old, poorly balanced swords, though, it was disconcerting how easily Kaeto and I fell into sync. He'd given me a startled sideways glance when I slotted myself in beside him—and nearly got his head sliced off for his trouble. But then he yielded his flank to me, clashing blades with the guard on the right while I took the one on the left.

The major downside to this was that it meant the other two men were going after Orlene. In the normal course of things, this might not have been an issue. Orlene didn't particularly like men, and when they pointed weapons in her face, that dislike tended to manifest as berserker rage with a lot of blood and lopped-off body parts involved.

But like the rest of us, she'd just come off a brutal two-day ride that had culminated with a couple of miles walking on foot. I heard her snarled curse over the ring of steel on steel, and my heart lurched with worry that she'd been injured. I couldn't afford to split my attention, though… a fact which very nearly got me killed a moment later.

The only warning I had that one of Orlene's opponents had successfully broken free of the fight was a whisper of air to my left. An instant before the third guard's sword would have sliced through the juncture of my neck and shoulder, Kaeto's blade whistled behind my head, missing me by an inch. Metal clashed as he turned the strike away, the parry leaving him wide open to the first guard's attack.

With a shout of dismay, I ducked under the second guard's wild swing to block a lunge that would have gutted the emperor like a fish. I kicked out, hoping to catch the man in the groin—but my exhaustion and the confusion of the fight meant I only landed a glancing blow to the top of his thigh.

"*Clear!*" Val shouted in Eburosi.

Instinct took over. I grabbed Kaeto and dragged him sideways and down, rolling both of us to the side where we ended up in a tangled heap. A flaming cloth bag flew through the air where we'd just been standing and hit one of the guards square in the breastplate.

The flimsy bag burst on impact, fine gray powder exploding out of it and instantly catching fire with a massive *whoosh*. The three guards who'd been attacking us screamed, dropping their swords to claw at their burned faces.

A cry came from Orlene's direction, the remaining guard falling to the ground with a wet gurgle as she took advantage of the confusion to run him through.

"What the *hell* was that?" Kaeto wheezed, his voice rising to a startled pitch.

I ignored him and pushed myself off his chest, grateful that he'd at least broken my fall. Shouts and hoofbeats were approaching from inside the imperial compound.

"Explanations later," Val said, hauling me to my feet and helping me get Kaeto upright as well.

"The horses?" I rasped, scanning the area. Tired as they were, they'd still bolted for safety when the firepowder had gone off.

"Over there," Orlene said, pushing me out of the way to haul Kaeto's arm over her broad shoulders.

I followed the jerk of her chin to see the horses milling together about fifty paces away. Val grabbed my arm as though he thought I needed support as well, and the four of us staggered toward the exhausted animals.

Fortunately, these horses had been the easiest ones to catch back in the raiders' valley — that's why we'd chosen them. Combined with the fact that they were nearly ready to drop after the journey, it meant that Val and I were able to grab the nearest two.

Orlene practically threw Kaeto into the saddle of the first horse and mounted the second horse herself. Val and I darted past them to grab the other two that were wearing saddles, climbing aboard just as the heavy gate started to rise with a labored clank of machinery, revealing reinforcements massing on the far side.

"Back to the southern district!" I ordered. "We'll ditch the horses and hide out there!"

"Assuming the horses don't drop from exhaustion before we make it," Orlene said grimly.

I spared a glance at Kaeto, hoping he'd just had the wind knocked out of him when we went down, as opposed to cracking ribs. He was hunched over his mount's neck, one arm wrapped around his ribcage. His lips pulled back in a grimace, but he yanked the horse around and put his heels to its sides.

The rest of us followed suit, the sound of horseshoes on cobbles ringing through the night. The two pack horses followed their herdmates into a reluctant canter, despite the fact that we hadn't taken the time to catch them.

It was no coincidence that the area around the imperial quarter was open and free of buildings. That, along with the high walls spaced at regular intervals with arrowslits, constituted the main defense against any invading armies bold enough to beard the Alyrion lion inside his den. The defending forces had cover; the approaching forces didn't.

That was bad for us, since it meant we had no place to hide until we made it farther into the city. And indeed, it took almost no time at all before pursuing hoofbeats clattered behind us—far too close for comfort. The guards would be riding fresh horses. There was no way we could outrun them.

I exchanged a questioning look with Val, who nodded grimly and reined his horse in, falling behind us.

"Be ready for your horses to bolt!" I called in Alyrion, mostly for Kaeto's benefit.

It took an alarmingly short time for Val to end up only a few lengths ahead of our pursuers.

"What do you—" Kaeto began, only for his words to be cut off when another fireball whooshed into life behind us. All three riding horses and the two pack animals leapt forward in startled flight, their exhaustion forgotten beneath their fear of the flames and noise.

When my mount stopped its frantic plunging and settled back into a canter, I chanced a look over my shoulder. The breath left my lungs in a relieved sigh when I made out Val still clinging to his horse, which appeared highly motivated to catch up to us.

Kaeto had lost a stirrup and was heaving himself back to a centered position in the saddle with his two-handed grip on the animal's mane, cursing fluently. Orlene was bent over her mount's neck to reduce wind resistance.

I braced for another firepowder bomb behind us, but none came. Val had set off the first one right in front of the pursuing guards, whose horses would have been thrown into utter confusion.

Their fresh mounts would be far more reactive to the explosion of flame than our exhausted ones.

Val caught up with us, and we continued as fast as we could through the towering edifices of the government district, back into the confusion of twisting streets and alleys that was the southern commerce district.

As soon as I saw a suitably dodgy looking alley off the main route of the Vaia Condora, I gestured for the others to follow me into it. The heaving breaths of the lathered horses echoed against the walls of the nearby buildings as we dismounted.

"We're ditching the horses," I said. "Take what you can carry, and don't leave anything incriminating behind. I think it's about a mile from here to the Vaia Meretricia. That's where we're going."

Kaeto, pale-faced with pain, growled, "Why there? That area is a seething pit of pagan malcontents."

I smiled broadly, aware that it probably looked more like a rictus. "Let's just say I know a brothel owner or two. We need a place to lie low."

EIGHTEEN

It wasn't ideal, but after some discussion, Orlene gave her hooded cloak to Kaeto. She was undeniably recognizable with her height and her head of braided red hair. But Val would be even *more* recognizable, and Kaeto was the one the guards were specifically looking out for.

As the physically strongest of us, Orlene also got saddled with supporting the injured emperor as he hobbled through the shadowed side streets with us, trying to avoid drawing attention without looking like we were skulking around suspiciously. I wasn't certain I'd ever witnessed two people who wanted to be touching each other less.

Orlene was a bit odd about people touching her at the best of times — especially people who also happened to be men. Meanwhile, Kaeto was... *Kaeto*. He was probably afraid that Orlene's Eburosi peasant-ness would rub off on him or something.

It didn't help that none of us had spent enough time exploring the twisting alleys of Amarius to have a reliable mental map beyond the main roads. We overshot the intersection that would have led us to the Vaia Meretricia and had to double back, reaching the Cock's Crow tavern shortly after the bells chimed one in the morning.

The tavern itself was closed at this hour, but fortunately, it wasn't the tavern I needed. It was the establishment located above it.

The two-story wooden building's unobtrusive side door was unlocked. It led us into a wide hallway dimly lit with oil lamps. The interior door directly across from the side entrance was firmly barred from the inside.

Kaeto took the opportunity to jerk his arm away from Orlene's broad shoulders in favor of steadying himself against the wall. "Are we to huddle in a hallway until the tavern owners find us in the morning and throw us out?"

The words were sour, and so was his expression. I wanted to channel my mother and warn him that his face would freeze like that—but realistically, if it were going to, it already would have done so years ago.

"You could always try telling them you're the true emperor, and that you'll have them beheaded unless they give you a free bowl of gruel as tribute," Orlene muttered, her tone equally acidic.

"There must be a stairway leading up to the second level," I said, already heading deeper into the building. "That's where we're going."

Sure enough, the hallway ended at a second door—this one with flickering light peeking through the gap at the bottom. Not having spent any time in Amarian brothels, I wasn't certain of the etiquette. I knocked lightly and turned the doorhandle. The unlocked door swung open beneath my touch on well-oiled hinges. It revealed an elegant receiving room populated by several girls wearing sheer white stolas and lounging artistically on the richly upholstered furniture.

"Ah," Kaeto said, not even bothering to lower his voice. "Not the hallway, then. Instead, I am expected to cower among whores."

An attractive teenage boy detached himself from a corner of the room and approached us. "If you didn't want whores, you prolly shouldn't have come to a brothel, mate. Will that be four for servicing tonight?" He looked between us, brows furrowing. "Or will you just be wanting to rent a couple of rooms by the hour?"

Kaeto visibly swelled with outrage next to me. "How *dare* you, you insolent whelp!"

The boy took a step back, raising his hands. "Oy! Didn't mean to offend, good sir. You'll find no judgment here, but I can't help you unless you tell me what it is you're after."

I resisted the urge to reach over and throttle the Alyrion emperor, in favor of grabbing him by the bicep and squeezing hard enough to make him hiss.

"Sorry about our companion, here," I said, ignoring the sense of Kaeto puffing up like an angry rooster beside me. "It's his first time, I'm sure he's just a bit nervous. Actually, we need to speak to either Saleene or Zuri. We can wait if they're, erm, otherwise engaged?"

I had no idea if the brothel's owners still saw clients of their own. I'd met the pair only once, back on Eburos, when they'd been visiting Caius and acting as unofficial envoys between the pagans of Amarius and the southern Eburosi port city of Rhyth.

It had been Caius who'd given me the address of the brothel and told me to go to them if I ever needed help in the capital. In hindsight, I probably should have approached the couple earlier, before things started imploding, to see if they remembered me and feel out their willingness to assist with my mission.

On the other hand, doing so would have given them the option to laugh at me outright and slam the door in my face. The pair had been embroiled — not entirely by choice — in the last Alyrion coup; the one that had put Kaeto on the throne in the first place. Their work with the pagans aside, it was quite likely that they wanted nothing more to do with imperial intrigue.

The lad's frown deepened, but he said, "I'll see if they're available." He turned to one of the girls decorating a low couch. "Marla, would you go and check for me? I can't leave the parlor unattended."

Marla made an unimpressed noise, but she peeled herself off the furniture and headed for a staircase at the back of the room, giving us a free show of her very attractive arse through shifting gauze as she left.

"I'll need your weapons, please," said the boy. "You can't go upstairs with 'em."

I obligingly unbuckled the sword belt I'd scavenged from the raider camp, sending a glare in Orlene's direction when she balked. Val gamely started handing over a seemingly never-ending collection of daggers and throwing knives from the depths of his loose clothing. I pulled out my various concealed shortblades as well, while Orlene relinquished her wickedly curved sword and parrying dagger.

Another glare, and Kaeto reluctantly disarmed along with the rest of us, until the poor teenager was almost comically overloaded with a pile of pointy objects. I didn't have the heart to tell him that Val still probably had at least one firepowder pouch in his possession that could burn this place to the ground before anyone could start grabbing buckets of water.

Happily, even if Saleene and Zuri *did* toss us out on our collective ears, malicious arson wasn't part of the plan.

Just as the boy was depositing the mass of metal and leather behind a counter in the corner, Marla returned. She leaned over the stair railing, looking down at us.

"Saleene says I'm supposed to bring you to her office. You'd better follow me."

I shared a glance with the others and headed up the staircase, my body feeling as though it had aged three decades in the last couple of days.

Told you horses are stupid, came a familiar mental voice. *I could've had you there in no time and burned down the palace gate for you when we arrived.*

Only because dragons don't understand the words 'international incident,' I thought back. Hopefully, I was successful at stifling the little voice in my head that whispered about how that didn't sound like such a bad idea right now.

Apparently, I hadn't been, since Xael only snorted.

Marla led us to the second level, and then down a hallway with rooms on either side, spaced at regular intervals. The exaggerated sounds of prostitutes pretending to enjoy sex came from behind several of the closed doors, and Kaeto made a barely audible noise of disgust.

"Exactly how well do you know these people?" Val asked, for my ears alone.

"Don't ask questions you don't want the answers to," I told him. "I'm sure it'll be fine, though."

Past the money-making part of the operation lay a larger room with communal tables and benches taking up much of the space. And beyond *that* lay a plain wooden door that lacked the carvings and ornamentation of the client rooms. Marla stopped in front of it and knocked.

"Yes, yes—show them in," came a muffled tenor voice from inside.

Marla cleared her throat and leaned close to me to murmur, "She's in a foul mood tonight, fair warning. And you should know that she doesn't like having her time wasted."

"Good to know," I said wryly. "It sounds like we'll get on quite well, in that case."

Marla opened the door and waved us into a space that would have been cramped for three people, let alone five. Every horizontal surface was piled high with scrolls, ledgers, and sheaves of unbound vellum. In combination with the lamps and candles illuminating the room, one wrong move felt like it might result in *accidental* arson, even if *malicious* arson was still off the table.

A tall, angular figure unfolded from behind the large desk near the far wall, brushing waves of thick black hair threaded with silver over one shoulder.

"What can I do for you?" Saleene asked, in the same no-nonsense, slightly impatient tones I remembered from our previous brief meeting. "If it's about unusual sexual predilections, Radil downstairs can get you sorted out—"

I stepped forward into a circle of brighter light, drawing breath to reintroduce myself and beg her help. Before I could, Kaeto dragged the hood of his cloak back almost violently, his gray eyes snapping fire.

"*You,*" he hissed, even as Saleene's eyes went wide.

She took a startled step back, nearly hitting the wall behind her. "*You!*" Then she seemed to rally. "Whatever the question is, the answer is *no!* Find another damn brothel—I'm not interested in getting pulled into another crusade, no matter *how* much of a grasping prick your younger brother is!"

I blinked, momentarily rendered speechless.

"You, uh, know each other personally, then?" I managed, looking between them.

"Sure sounds like it," Orlene muttered from behind me.

"This *godless heathen* was part of the insurrectionist army that captured me after I fled Proclus' assassination attempt!" Kaeto snapped.

Apparently uncowed by the presence of a deposed emperor in her office, Saleene leaned forward, hands flat on her desk, and *glared*. "The *same* army that helped install you on your older brother's throne, *Your Imperial Majesty*," she snapped back.

I raised a finger like a student seeking the tutor's attention. "If we could maybe back up a bit...?"

Saleene's gaze — a darker and stormier shade of gray than Kaeto's — pinned me. Her eyes narrowed. "Wait a minute. I recognize you! You're from Eburos! Holy gods... is *Caius* behind this mess somehow? Didn't that old fool learn his lesson about playing dice with the Alyrion throne the *last time*?"

On hearing Caius' name, Kaeto inhaled sharply.

I resisted the urge to wince and slap a hand over my face to cover it. I'd been extremely careful not to let slip anything about my connection to the former palace advisor, knowing any mention of him in front of Kaeto would be akin to waving a red flag in front of a bull.

"*What* did you just say?" Kaeto demanded in a dangerous tone.

To say that he and Caius hadn't parted on the best of terms was a disservice to understatement. Caius had, at one point, made a spirited attempt to put Kaeto's shapeshifting pagan half-brother on the throne instead of him. Afterward, Kaeto had made an equally spirited attempt to have the pair assassinated as they fled by sea to Eburos.

Invoking Caius' name and implying he might have something to do with the current coup was not, as they say, serving our immediate goals.

Oops.

"Oh, good," Val said, sounding as unutterably weary as I suddenly felt. "Now it's *all* kicking off."

NINETEEN

Kaeto, Saleene, and I all started talking at once. Or rather, I was talking. They were yelling—which meant that my contribution disappeared beneath the noise.

I caught Orlene's eye before things could escalate from verbal to physical evisceration. Orlene shot me a sour look, but she pushed past me to stand in the middle of the room and bellow, "*Quiet!*"

It was a bellow that had been honed on battlefields and training fields alike, and it was considerably more impressive than either mine or Valeph's.

It worked.

According to Caius, Saleene the brothel owner had once been Salieri the mercenary soldier. Reacting immediately and instinctively to parade-ground bellows tended to be a rather important aspect of that line of work. Meanwhile, Kaeto was probably just in shock that anyone would dare yell at him to shut up.

They both turned to gape at Orlene. I took advantage of the lull to step in front of her and regain the room's attention.

"Right. So," I began, aware that I hadn't actually figured out how to de-escalate the situation before I'd opened my mouth. I cleared my throat. "It's true that Caius is a mutual acquaintance, but he has nothing to do with us being here."

Not strictly accurate, since Caius was the one who'd told me how to find Saleene and Zuri if I needed help, but... *details*.

"Valeph, Orlene and I are here because we heard there were stolen dragon eggs in Amarius," I went on gamely. "Kaeto is here because while I was attempting to get information from him, someone inconveniently decided to try and capture—or possibly assassinate—him. So now we're trying to get his throne back while *also* finding the dragon eggs."

Saleene stared at me... for, like, a *really* long time.

Finally, she blinked. "And you're all in my brothel now, *because*...?"

"Because the guards at the gates of the imperial quarter have orders to capture or kill Kaeto and anyone with him on sight. Which, um, we found out the hard way about an hour ago."

Saleene's gaze narrowed. "That is *not* an answer to the question I asked."

There was no good way to sugarcoat this next part for Kaeto's benefit. "We're here because Caius said I should come to you and Zuri if I was in danger. He said you'd help."

The office door swung open, revealing a dark-skinned woman with short-cropped hair in the doorway. "What's going on in here?" The newcomer demanded in a pronounced Kulawi accent. "I heard shouting."

Then her gaze fastened on Kaeto and she froze.

Saleene sighed in clear disgust. "Zuri, my love. I'm *so* glad you're here. We appear to have a new problem."

～～❦～～

After a quick recap of the relevant facts, Zuri sagged back against the wall next to the door. "Well, that's put us right back in the shit; now, hasn't it?" she said.

I was beginning to worry about the fact that Kaeto hadn't started yelling again. His face had a pale, pinched look that I didn't much like. It was the sort of look someone might get after riding almost nonstop for two days, being thrown unexpectedly into a sword battle, and then walking a mile on a half-healed leg injury in the middle of the night.

I'd turned over the attempts at diplomacy to Valeph, since he was better at it anyway. He'd been a *terrible* priest by all accounts, but some aspects of his previous life had stuck with him, nonetheless. Talking to people without immediately pissing them off was one of the skills that had transferred successfully to secular life.

"You mentioned the younger brother, Bruccias," he was saying. "He is the person behind the coup?"

"He marched in with an army, claiming this one was dead," Zuri said warily, tilting her chin to indicate Kaeto. "In the absence of an imperial heir, he's next in line for the throne. According to the gossip, it didn't require much persuasion for the court to let him take the reins, at least provisionally."

"And once they let him get a proverbial foot in the door, he wasted no time in ousting anyone in the palace who showed loyalty to Kaeto, and replacing them with his own men," Saleene added dryly.

"I see," Val said. "We regret bringing trouble to your doorstep. However, I'm certain you can understand the gravity of our situation. May we prevail upon you for safe haven tonight? The emperor's face is well known in the city. Our options are limited."

"As far as compelling arguments for why I shouldn't tell you all to go fuck yourselves, I've heard better," Saleene said.

I drew breath to reply, but Zuri got in before me.

"You say Bruccias' guards from the palace pursued you?" she asked.

"We lost them in the southern quarter," I said quickly.

"Which only means he'll have men out searching the area for you," Saleene snapped. "Now that he knows Kaeto is back in Amarius, Bruccias can't afford to have him running around at large." She eyed Kaeto's pasty face with a look of intense irritation. "Though the 'running around' part might be optimistic, from the look of things."

"You are flirting with treason, you unnatural pagan harlot—" Kaeto took an aggressive step forward with his bad leg. The remaining blood drained from his already pasty complexion. He gasped, his eyes rolling up behind the lids, and crumpled slowly toward the floor.

I was already in motion, lunging forward to grab him before he could faceplant on one of the overburdened tables. I realized two things in quick succession—first, that the bastard was surprisingly heavy, and second, that everyone else seemed perfectly happy to let him brain himself on the furniture.

I ended up half-pinned beneath his limp body on the floorboards, the breath knocked out of me. "Hey, thanks so much for the help, everyone," I wheezed.

"Hmm," Zuri said philosophically. "Now I suppose we'll *have* to let them stay the night."

"The next time I see Caius," Saleene muttered, "I will kill that man in the most painful and imaginative way possible."

⚜

We ended up borrowing two of the unused client rooms. Orlene and Val were in one, where they were ostensibly trying to get a few hours of rest before we figured out what to do next. I was in the other with Kaeto, who'd been deposited on the bed, still unresponsive after his earlier faint.

I'd wrestled his layers off, leaving him in only his smallclothes. The lamps in the room had not been arranged with medical care in mind, but even in the low, moody lighting, I could see the problem well enough.

Sheer exhaustion and stress might have been the main culprit behind Kaeto's collapse, but the massive expanse of bruising across the right side of his back and ribcage probably wasn't helping matters.

Part of it was sickly yellow-green and brown—a memento of when I'd dragged him off his horse in the ravine, or possibly when Xael had shaken him off his back in the valley. The old bruises were partially overlaid with new ones painted in gaudy black and blue, fresh from the fight at the palace when I'd tackled him to get him out of Val's line of fire.

I took advantage of his unconsciousness to press on his ribs one by one. Nothing shifted in a way that would indicate a break, but I wouldn't be at all surprised if a couple of them were cracked. He'd probably benefit from having them wrapped, but that would be a lot easier to do while he was sitting up.

The room was supplied with a basin of water, so I contented myself with sponging him off as best I could.

The knee didn't honestly look too bad, though I was sure it hurt like hell. That, I did wrap, using bandages Zuri had dropped off at the same time she brought in a bowl of stew for me.

Of the pair, Zuri seemed slightly more sympathetic to our plight. I wasn't entirely sure what to expect in the morning—whether Saleene would throw us out to take our chances on the street, or allow us more time to cobble together some sort of plan.

I'd just finished pulling off the ill-fitting tunic I'd looted from the raider's camp, and I was making a half-hearted attempt to sponge the travel grime from my body with the cloudy water left in the basin when a low groan came from the bed.

I turned around, not terribly concerned by my uncovered breasts, since Kaeto had already seen me half-naked and frigging myself not long after we first met. The erstwhile emperor of Alyrios grunted and flailed into a sitting position, only to gasp as his injuries made themselves known.

"It's all right," I said. "We're safe. You fainted."

Kaeto blinked at me in the low lamplight, one arm wrapped around his bruised ribs as he panted in pain.

"I am the ruler… of an empire… spanning continents," he said through gritted teeth. "I do not *faint*."

It would have sounded more impressive if he hadn't been breathless from pain.

"Uh-huh," I told him. "Sure. So, anyway, you abruptly decided to take a much-needed nap. At which point, Saleene and Zuri agreed to let us stay the night. Presumably, that was because no one wanted to haul you down the stairs, and I guess tossing you out of a convenient window would have attracted too much attention."

I could see he wanted to argue about it some more, and I was somewhat surprised when he didn't. Instead, he was quiet for several moments.

"We have no actionable strategy for removing my brother from the throne," he said eventually.

I turned around and resumed washing off the road dust. "Not… as such, no. Although, if

Bruccias is claiming you're dead, then it seems like showing up alive would be a good start."

Kaeto shifted position in the bed, sheets rustling. "The unnatural harlot who owns this place is unfortunately correct. Now that Bruccias knows I am here, he will devote every resource at his disposal to finding and eliminating me."

Yeah, he probably would, at that.

"We need to find and consolidate any forces that are still loyal to you," I said, letting the sponge fall back in the basin with a small splash. "Even if he's taken over the palace guard, surely he can't have purged the entire city guard in such a short time."

"Perhaps not," Kaeto allowed. "But contacting them will be risky. He may have placed spies among them, or—"

The muffled sound of crashing and shouting filtered up to us from the ground floor. Heavy bootsteps pounded up the stairs, mingled with feminine shouts of dismay and anger.

"Search every room!" came a deep male voice. "Kick down the doors if you have to!"

"Fuck!" I cursed.

Kaeto lunged to his feet, only to catch himself on the bedframe when his legs refused to hold him. "Weapons!" he hissed.

"Downstairs," I reminded him. "Val might still have a firepowder pouch hidden away, but…"

I trailed off, because he probably wouldn't set fire to the building we were all currently trapped inside, along with a bunch of innocent prostitutes and customers.

The sound of doors crashing open at the far end of the hall reached us. My mind raced in circles. The window? No, Kaeto would never be able to climb out from the second story in his current condition. I glanced down, suddenly far too aware that my boobs were on display.

Except... *oh*. My breath caught.

"Get back on the bed and follow my lead," I said, fumbling for the knot of the drawstring holding my too-large trousers up. "And I swear to the gods, if you make a fuss about this, I will smack you upside the head so hard that you won't even notice when the guards barge in and kill us."

156

TWENTY

Kaeto gaped at me as I tore at the knot of my makeshift belt and shimmied out of my remaining clothing. Then he looked down at himself, as though only now realizing that he'd been stripped to his linen braies.

His attention flicked to me again, then to the room's only door, and back to me. "You intend to—"

I crossed the space separating us, shoved him onto the bed, and climbed on top of him. "You're damned right I do." Tugging a blanket free, I dragged it up far enough to hopefully hide Kaeto's low-slung undergarments from view. "I'd say something about your virtue being safe with me, but—no, shut up. They're here."

He'd drawn breath to say *something*, but the thudding footsteps were right outside the door. I slapped a palm over his mouth to prevent him from blurting anything stupid while the men outside might hear. Then I grabbed the wrist of the arm he raised to fend me off, slamming it down on the mattress above his head and pinning it there.

In a twist I definitely *hadn't* seen coming, Kaeto bucked beneath me—his cock springing to attention between us so abruptly that he was lucky he didn't faint again when half his blood moved abruptly south.

"Open up!" came a deep, muffled voice, followed by a fist pounding heavily against the wood.

"Oooh!" I moaned, ridiculously loudly. "Oh, *yes*, Daddy! You're so deep! *Give it to me harder!*"

The erection grinding against the crease of my inner thigh flagged at that, which was honestly a bit reassuring, because *eww*. Still, the satisfying combination of shock, outrage, and a tiny sliver of fear swirling in Kaeto's gray gaze might almost make up for the prospect of being horribly murdered while pretending to bump uglies.

"Yes, *yes!*" I squealed, rolling my hips against his like someone trying to stay with a runaway horse. "Oh my god, *don't stop!*"

Wood splintered as the doorframe gave way beneath a solid kick. I manufactured a scream of surprise, playing the unlikely role of a professional whore who'd been too lost in pleasure to notice the sound of guards breaking down doors along the hall.

Both Kaeto and I craned around to stare wide-eyed at the intruders as two very large men in palace livery shouldered into the room. I kept my hand clamped firmly over Kaeto's mouth, muffling whatever words were trying to escape.

Incriminating ones, probably.

"What are you doing in here?" I shrieked. "*Get out!* Some of us are trying to make a *living*, you perverts!"

Unfortunately, the men didn't seem fazed by my contrived hysterics. They scanned the room as though expecting someone else to be hiding in the corner. The taller guard pointed at Kaeto and said, "That one kind of fits the description."

Kaeto made another muffled noise of outrage, and I squeezed the tendons of the wrist I was pinning until he shut up. His hips bucked beneath me again, as though he couldn't control the reaction. I experienced the sobering realization that it would have felt really good, if not for the whole *'possibility of imminent death'* thing.

"*What description?*" I demanded, still in my best *'shrill harpy'* voice.

They continued to ignore me.

The broader one shook his head. "Nah, everyone knows that little prick is impotent. Always pretending to have a mistress, but none of 'em ever get pregnant."

Beneath me, Kaeto had stopped squirming and gone very still.

The taller guard shrugged. "And no legitimate heir in sight. Yeah, you're right." He sniggered, directing a sneer at the man I was pinning. "Can you imagine? An emperor letting a woman take charge in bed!"

Broad Guard chuckled. "If he got caught like this, he'd probably *beg* to be executed." For the first time, he addressed Kaeto directly. "Ah, well. Don't feel too bad, mate. At least you can get it up with the right, er, *persuasion.*"

Tall Guard's smirk said he was having trouble keeping his laughter under control. "Have a *lovely* evening, friend," he managed. "*So* sorry to interrupt."

His gaze traveled down to where we would have been joined if this had been real, pausing there significantly for a moment before the two burst into guffaws of laughter and withdrew, swinging the door closed to the extent the broken frame allowed.

I didn't move, partly because I didn't want to risk anything giving the game away before they were well and truly gone… and partly because I was at a bit of a loss when it came to transitioning from *'borderline sexual assault, with a side of brutal humiliation by complete strangers,'* to whatever passed for normal between a deposed emperor and his erstwhile kidnapper.

So, we stayed there, unmoving, for what felt like a ludicrously long time while the last few doors were kicked open. The process culminated in some truly creative insults and cursing from Saleene. They must have reached her office at the end of the hall. I winced, picturing the precarious stacks of ledgers and scrolls covering every available surface in the room.

Beneath me, I wasn't entirely sure Kaeto was even breathing—which seemed like it could be problematic given how long it took before the guards' bootsteps finally receded. Around us, the brothel went ominously quiet. I peeled my hand away from Kaeto's face and sat up.

He licked his lips slowly. I could see words gathering in his throat, only to be discarded. The silence dragged.

"We will never speak of this again," he said eventually.

I nodded. "Yes, that sounds like a good—"

The door creaked open on bent hinges, revealing a livid Saleene. Her snapping eyes took in the scene, a muscle ticking in her angular jaw.

"Oh. So that's how you managed it," she said, biting off the words. "Good thing the guards were idiots, then."

"Yeah, we've just decided that we're not talking about this. Ever," I told her. "I'm, uh, really sorry about your broken doors, by the way. Are Orlene and Val all right? I assume we would have heard the commotion if they weren't."

"They're my next stop," Saleene grated, as though every word had personally offended her.

It occurred to me that I was still straddling Kaeto's thighs, though at least I'd slid down a few inches so we'd both have plausible deniability regarding whether he was hard or not. Although, if he was still hard after all *that*, we might be entering some '*unusual sexual predilection*' territory that even *I* would have a difficult time accommodating.

So, you're planning on accommodating him at some point in the future? asked a familiar voice in my head.

I stifled a groan. *Oh, my gods, Xael—please shut the fuck up. Because you are* not *helping right now.*

In no world was I picturing Kaeto pinned beneath me, tied to the bed, writhing and gasping through a gag as I rode him to completion.

Clearly not, Xael deadpanned.

It was at approximately this point that I realized I *still* hadn't climbed off Kaeto's body, and both he and Saleene were giving me narrow, judgmental looks.

I cleared my throat. "Sorry. Could, uh, could someone grab my clothes, please?"

Saleene raised an eyebrow. "You're in a brothel. Clothing service costs extra." At which point, she turned on her heel and disappeared into the hallway.

This left me to clamber off the bed and perform the walk-of-not-very-much-shame to the corner where I'd piled our clothing. I carefully avoided eye contact as I gathered Kaeto's clothes and tossed them onto the bed, then pulled on my own poorly fitting stolen garb.

Maybe the rush of narrowly avoiding death for the second time in a day had lent Kaeto a burst of strength, because when I cautiously glanced around a couple of minutes later, he was dressed and standing under his own power.

I opened my mouth for some purpose that might or might not involve the insertion of my left foot, but Kaeto beat me to it.

"We should check on your comrades," he said gruffly, and brushed past me to the damaged door.

I shut my mouth with a click and followed his limping stride, confident that we'd have heard if they were hauled off, but concerned for other reasons. Kaeto stopped in the doorway of the room next to ours. I pushed past him to find Saleene and Val at the shuttered window. Val was bare to the waist and wearing a lacy half-veil over the lower part of his face, in the style of women in southwest Utrea, near the coast. His long, silver hair was artfully arranged over both shoulders to obscure the flatness of his chest.

"Where's Orlene?" I demanded, my pulse spiking.

"Either right outside the window or lying in a heap in the alley, two stories down," Val said grimly. He rapped on the right shutter with his knuckles and opened it a couple of seconds later, while Saleene opened the other one.

I rushed forward and stuck my head out, craning around until I saw a dark shape clinging to the wall a few feet away.

"All clear," Val said, and Orlene grunted.

She was wearing Val's black cloak to help her blend into the alley's dark shadows, in the unlikely event that anyone thought to look up. Her strong hands were curled around the edge of the building's flat roof, while the toes of her boots balanced precariously on a horizontal board running along the bottom of the wall's line of second story windows.

At Val's words, she started shuffling toward us, until she was able to stretch out one long leg around the obstruction of the open shutter and get a foot on the windowsill. I wrapped an arm around her thigh to steady her while she got her center of mass past the shutter, then Val and I took her weight as she swung her lower body into the room and let go her grip on the roof-edge.

We managed to get her inside without ending up in a tangle on the floor, while Kaeto and Saleene looked on in bewilderment.

"Wouldn't it have been easier for *you* to play the role of the working girl?" Saleene asked Orlene, as Val stripped off the half-veil and tossed it aside with distaste.

Val's expression, usually affable and difficult to read, had grown stony. "No," he said, answering for her. "It really wouldn't have."

Orlene, meanwhile, had the same air of never wanting to talk about this night again as Kaeto.

Val's pale, angry eyes slipped to me. "How did you two manage to trick them? They must've had a description to go off, like the guards at the imperial gate."

"Misdirection," I said tersely, ignoring Saleene's barely audible snort in the background. "Plus, as I'm sure you noticed, they weren't very bright."

"True." Val grabbed his loose tunic and over-robe, shrugging into the concealing clothing. "So, now what?"

Zuri poked her head in. "No one's hurt. They didn't seem interested in anything except finding this one." She gestured at Kaeto. "Most of the customers were just happy not to be detained by the guards, but a couple demanded refunds. I gave them half."

"Wonderful," Saleene said in a flat tone.

"What's almost more worrying to me is the idea that they're trashing businesses indiscriminately," Zuri went on. "This was part of a sweep. If they'd had information that their target was here, they would have done a more thorough job searching."

It was a good point.

"Yes," Saleene agreed. "That thought had occurred to me, too."

"This district is a haven for pagans and pagan sympathizers," Kaeto said. "My *dear* younger brother doesn't like pagans any more than my older brother did. I doubt he's concerned about damages to pagan-run businesses."

Zuri's face grew pinched. Saleene's expression was grim.

Before Kaeto's successful coup against his older brother Proclus, the city had been on the brink of a massive pogrom against anyone who worshipped the Old Gods—one that would have spilled out to the rest of the empire in short order if left unchecked. I was sure neither Zuri nor Saleene were in a hurry to return to those days.

I met Zuri's dark gaze. "This is why we need to get him back on the throne," I said quietly.

"And you intend to do that *how*, exactly?" Saleene asked, in a voice that could strip paint. "In case you haven't noticed, he can barely stand up."

Amazingly, Kaeto didn't have anything to say to this. Both he and Orlene had been disturbingly quiet, in fact. But I couldn't worry about either of them now—not in that way.

"The previous plan still stands," I said. "We need to consolidate forces that are still loyal to Kaeto. Bruccias clearly had this whole thing planned in detail, but he can't have wiped out every bit of loyalist support in such a short amount of time."

Saleene made an unhappy noise. "As much as I hate to say it, you're right. We can't go back to how things were before." She sighed heavily. "All right. I know a place you can hide where the guards won't find you... but you're *really* not going to like it."

TWENTY-ONE

Acouple of hours later, I was forced to concede that Saleene had been correct. I *really* didn't like this. Her much-touted *'place where the guards wouldn't find us'* had ended up being… *catacombs.*

And not just *any* catacombs. No, *these* catacombs appeared to be constructed using human bones as building materials, for the gods' sake. Because why make your corridors and arches out of bricks or timber when you could use skulls and femurs instead?

Yeesh.

Val, the former priest, had stopped cold when our oil lanterns first illuminated the stacks and stacks of empty eye sockets staring out at us from the walls.

"Wh-what?" he stammered, and I wasn't sure I'd ever seen him so wrong-footed. "Are those skulls… *human?*"

"Yes," Saleene said grimly, not sounding thrilled about it herself.

Val's colorless eyes jerked to land on Kaeto, flashing pinkish red in the lamplight like an animal's. "But that's *barbaric!* Why were these people not given proper funerals and their remains cremated? There are hundreds of them! *Thousands!*"

Kaeto stared at him like he was an imbecile, and I braced myself for full-on cultural warfare.

"Tens of thousands, I daresay. Do you have any idea how much fuel it would take to cremate that many bodies?"

"Alyrions bury their corpses rather than burning them," Zuri said, lifting her lantern to play its light over the geometric patterns of bone overhead. "But in cities as big and old as Amarius, they eventually run out of space. At some point, someone decided this would be a good alternative."

Orlene craned up to look at the corbeled ceiling above us. "It's gruesome, certainly. But I suppose there's a kind of grim artistry to it as well."

It was the most she'd said at one time since we'd left the brothel. I wanted to get her alone so I could ask if she was all right, but it didn't seem as though that was going to be in the cards anytime soon.

"I wasn't aware you even realized these tunnels existed, *Your Majesty*," Saleene said. Even now, she appeared constitutionally incapable of keeping sarcastic resentment from creeping into her tone when addressing Kaeto directly.

"You think I'm unaware of the catacombs beneath my own capital?" Kaeto shot back. "You pagans inhabited them like cockroaches during my brother's persecution. Half of the city guard was too superstitious to set foot inside them. It caused him no end of trouble."

"Good," Zuri said, with feeling.

The warren of tunnels must have been extensive. According to Zuri, access was available via a number of secret entrances hidden in old buildings scattered around the commerce district. The one we'd used had been just across the street from the building housing the Cock's Crow and the brothel. It was little more than a hole in the foundation, strewn with rubble leading sharply downward into the inky blackness of this eerie, underground world.

No effort had been made to arrange the chunks of stone and concrete into usable stairs, and Kaeto had mumbled curses as he navigated the precarious climb down the collapsed pile on his bad leg.

I wasn't sure if I agreed with Saleene's assessment of the catacombs as a safe haven for the four of us. After all, if Kaeto knew about their existence, it followed that Bruccias did as well.

Still, I supposed that the logistics of actually searching them made it impractical for a man who was already busy trying to consolidate power that rightfully belonged to someone else. Aside from the guards' unwillingness to enter in the first place, any intruders would be audible from some distance away as they approached through the echoing spaces.

All we'd have to do would be to hide in the nearest convenient nook and extinguish our lights. Anyone searching would most likely blunder right past us if we stayed quiet. There were worse bolt holes, even if I suspected I'd never be able to sleep again without visions of blank-eyed skulls watching me.

I shuddered.

"There's a stash of supplies in a vault not too far ahead," Zuri said, venturing deeper into the twisting maze. "Sometimes the rats get into them, but the elders make sure they're checked and replenished regularly."

Right. Because of course there were going to be rats involved.

Stringy, Xael mused. *And small. But not bad if you're hungry enough.*

Trust me, I'm not that hungry, I thought back, making a face.

"You do realize," Saleene said tartly, "that we're basically spilling all of our strategic secrets to the enemy."

That brought my attention back to my surroundings with a snap.

"Surely the enemy is Bruccias," I said.

Kaeto made a disgruntled noise. "Have I behaved so abominably toward the pagans during my reign, to draw your ire in such a way?" he snapped.

"No," Zuri said firmly, shooting Saleene a quelling look. "You haven't."

"Maybe not," Saleene agreed, her tone still poisonous. "Instead, you tried to have Caius and your half-brother killed after they basically handed you the throne on a silver platter."

I held my breath, still not convinced that we wouldn't have to drag these two off each other at some point.

Kaeto stared at Saleene as though she were a puzzle he couldn't work out. "And my understandable desire to secure the throne against a potential pretender is honestly more important to you than the fact that I negotiated peace with the pagans, and then enforced it against the radical Deimonist religious backlash?"

"He wasn't a *pretender*," Saleene said. "He was your father's rightful heir."

Kaeto snorted. "Yes. And how would that have ended up? An artless half-Kulawi pagan commoner—one who spent half his life in a *prison cell*—sitting on the Alyrion throne?"

"We'll never know," Saleene snarled, "because he didn't *want* your bloody throne in the first place."

"Maybe we should focus on the person who *does* want the bloody throne," I suggested hopefully.

To my surprise, it worked.

Kaeto grunted, not returning Saleene's last verbal salvo.

"You're right," Zuri said. "If Bruccias is going to start up pagan persecution again, he's our biggest concern right now."

"Which returns us to the question of what to do next," Val muttered. He was still eyeing the bone-walls with deep misgivings, but his point was a practical one.

"The city guard," I said, relieved to move the conversation on to more productive topics. "How loyal would you say they are?"

There was a pause, silence settling over the corridor except for our quiet footfalls and the soft sound of breathing.

"Let's just say I only had to execute a handful of them after disposing of my older brother and taking his place." Kaeto sounded grim.

I winced. "So, not very. Still, that was a different situation. You're not dead. Bruccias is holding the throne illegally, right? Wouldn't that mean something to them?"

"It would only take one greedy guard to run to the palace and rat him out," Val said. "You can bet there's a hefty reward for information leading to his capture or death."

"No doubt," Kaeto said tartly.

"Let's keep moving. The vault is just through this archway," Zuri said, leading the way into a much larger space. Her voice echoed off the distant walls and ceiling. "For now, let's just worry about—"

She stopped so abruptly that the rest of us nearly ran into her. Ahead of us, the edges of our combined lantern light illuminated a large group of robed individuals, several of whom were holding sharpened wooden spears and rough, homemade bows pointed at us.

"Son of a *bitch*!" Orlene snarled, drawing steel.

Kaeto and I were right behind her when it came to grabbing for weapons, while next to us, Val fumbled for his remaining firepowder pouch.

"Oh, you have *got* to be kidding me," Saleene muttered.

"Don't move!" shouted one of the cloaked figures. "If you want to live, drop your weapons and kneel on the floor with your hands on your heads!"

TWENTY-TWO

"**S**top!" Zuri cried, stepping forward and raising her hands palm out toward the gathered figures. She reached up and dragged her hood back, baring her face. "We're pagans!"

I suspected Kaeto might have something to say about that, but while the erstwhile emperor of Alyrios was many things, he wasn't a fool. There was a tense pause, broken only by low murmurs from a few of the armed group ahead of us.

"Stay where you are!" called the apparent spokesperson.

The scrape of flint-strikers and the slide of metal against metal reached us as people lit lamps and opened the shutters on dark lanterns. Light flooded the shadowy vault, illuminating a ragtag group of perhaps fifteen people. I steadied my grip on my sword hilt, aware that our only chance if violence erupted would be Val's firepowder bomb.

The leader of the armed group studied Zuri for a moment before pushing back his own hood. He was older than I would have expected from his voice.

"I recognize you," he said, lifting a quelling hand to gesture at the crowd behind him. "I've seen you at meetings."

The tension eased a bit as people lowered their makeshift weapons, though they still watched us warily. Following a hunch, I sheathed my sword with slow, exaggerated movements.

"Put your weapons away," I told the others under my breath.

Orlene made a wordless, unconvinced noise, but she returned her sword to her belt. Val pocketed the cloth pouch and flint he'd been holding in readiness. Kaeto hesitated a moment longer, but then he, too, slid his sword into its scabbard.

Saleene stepped forward, warily lowering her hood as she joined Zuri. "We're seeking sanctuary from the forces commanded by Bruccias. Is that why you're here as well?"

The man stepped forward to meet them. "Yes, that's right. Palace guards descended on the Southern Quarter and began ransacking pagan businesses. Rumors spread that Bruccias was resuming the pogrom against us, so we fled here to regroup and plan. Forgive the inhospitable welcome, sisters."

"No forgiveness is needed," Zuri said without hesitation. "We should share what we know and make plans. There may not be enough supplies down here to handle a large-scale flight into the catacombs."

A middle-aged woman with dull brown hair and weathered features stepped up to join the older man. "There aren't," she said grimly. "We've grown complacent under the emperor Kaeto's rule, convincing ourselves that something like this couldn't happen again."

Kaeto limped forward into the brighter light before I could move to stop him.

"Yes," he said, "About that..."

Orlene let out another unhappy growl, and I could sympathize. Flouting Kaeto's true identity to a group of pagans we didn't know would *not* have been my first choice in this situation.

"Oh," Saleene said. "So, we're doing it this way, I guess?"

Zuri recovered quicker. "Ah. Yes. As it happens, we do have a particular reason for needing to hide from Bruccias' guards. May I present the emperor Kaeto—who, I will remind you, negotiated the truce between the Deimonists and our own pagan brethren."

There was nothing quiet about the confusion of startled voices that rose in response to her words.

"Please, don't trouble yourself to kneel," Kaeto said tartly.

The man and woman who'd been speaking for the group peered at Kaeto with clear misgivings.

"Forgive me," the man said, "but we have been reliably informed that the emperor Kaeto was killed by raiders in the mountains west of the River Uvi."

"Not so much killed as severely irked." Kaeto bit off the words. "My treacherous younger brother is plotting to take my throne. If he is allowed to hold it, prepare yourself for the coming of a second Proclus... only with considerably less drunkenness and considerably more guile."

The man and the woman shared a look of alarm, while behind them, the rest of the group went quiet. Kaeto's older brother Proclus had, by all reports, been a drunken lout—but he'd also dreamed of using his people's irrational fear and hatred of pagans to turn the empire outward to conquest once more.

The theft of the dragon eggs had led the rulers of Eburos and Utrea to conclude that Kaeto might be harboring his own dreams of fresh conquest. Now, it seemed far more likely that Bruccias was the one turning his vision toward the free nations to the north and west. In which case, I sincerely hoped these people appreciated the fact that Kaeto was their best bet to maintain peace and safety in Alyrios.

An old woman hobbled up to Kaeto from the rear of the group, her hunched back bent nearly double. She peered up at him with rheumy eyes, her wrinkled brow knitting in concentration.

"This is the emperor," she proclaimed. "I've seen him many times over the years, when he rode past my shop as part of the royal retinue."

"Thank you, madame," Kaeto said, with more civility than I would have given him credit for.

And that was something I needed to be careful of… because Kaeto might be a vicious arsehole in private, but he was also a skilled diplomat. He'd knitted a crumbling empire back together nearly singlehandedly, using little more than the strength of his own charisma.

The pair of pagan leaders exchanged another speaking look, then both of them bowed low.

"Your Imperial Majesty," said the man. "You humble us with your presence. We know how much of an ally you have been to our people in recent years. How may we be of service to you?"

The tension in Kaeto's spine eased. "First, you can dispense with the bowing and scraping. We are not at court, and I require assistance more than I require abasement. Bruccias is aware of my presence in the capital. My... *esteemed allies—*"

Saleene made a tiny, barely audible choked noise.

"—suggested that the catacombs would make an effective bolt hole."

The elderly woman snorted. "They were right enough, if you don't mind living like a rat in a sewer."

"That is the next challenge," Kaeto agreed. "Hiding in the dark will not remove my brother from the throne. Is the city guard still loyal, or has Bruccias corrupted them, as well as the palace guard?"

"I've heard no reports of the city guard harassing anyone," the female leader said, though her tone was uncertain.

"More than usual, you mean?" Saleene asked.

"She's right," said the man. "Many in the city guard still harbor resentment toward pagans, even if the current laws constrain them from acting on it openly."

My stomach sank. "It would only take one rotten apple in the barrel to give up your location to Bruccias, if we tried to go to them."

"What other option is there?" Val asked.

I had an answer, but it wasn't going to be a simple one. "Heleva. We need to get out of the city and go to Heleva."

Kaeto shot me a glance sharp enough to slice through bone. I frowned back at him, not sure what that look was supposed to mean.

"There's a garrison stationed there," I went on. "And once we're clear of the capital, we have... other resources we can draw on."

Oh, I'm a 'resource' now, am I? Fortunately, Xael sounded more amused than irritated.

It's not like I can blurt out that we have dragons to every group of strangers we meet inside the creepy skull-tunnel, I sent.

"That's not a bad idea," Orlene said. "Assuming we can get out of Amarius without being captured."

More conversation erupted in the main group. Then a woman spoke up.

"My brother's family runs a freight business out of the city port. He might be able to smuggle you out, but you'd have to take the river route. There isn't much traffic on the Uvi in summertime."

The reason for that was a good one. The river valley during the warm season was a seething mass of insect-borne pestilence.

"I dislike the idea of leaving the capital," Kaeto said. "It smacks of abscondment."

"And staying here helps us how, exactly?" I prodded.

"She's right," Saleene said in a monotone. "I'd be thrilled if you all went as far away as possible."

"Don't listen to her," Zuri said. "She's no happier at the prospect of Bruccias on the throne than the rest of us. So, can we arrange this? What needs to happen to get the four of them on a barge heading south?"

The others fell into intense conversation with the young woman who had the freight-hauling connections. Meanwhile, Kaeto continued to watch me with an intense frown on his face that I couldn't quite parse.

"We're still going to be stuck down here for some time," Val murmured, distracting me from the puzzle. "We should try to get some rest... although, given our surroundings, *restful* is not the word that springs immediately to mind." He ran a gimlet eye over the walls of old bones surrounding us.

"Yes," I agreed, shaking myself free of my rumination. "We're exhausted and battered. Best to use the time we're given to recover our strength."

Unfortunately, that would also give me far too much time to mull over the decision I would have to make soon. I'd been sent here with the others to recover or destroy the stolen eggs by whatever means necessary. But I didn't think the people in charge had expected '*whatever means necessary*' to extend to directly intervening in an Alyrion coup... especially if that intervention included using full-grown battle dragons directly in service of Emperor Kaeto.

TWENTY-THREE

One thing no one mentioned about underground environments was how cold and damp they could be. At least, it certainly felt that way to my exhausted, summer-adapted body.

The stash of supplies in the vault was woefully inadequate for the number of people sheltering here, which meant not enough food and not enough blankets. The man and woman who seemed to be in charge—Iovis and Alcimene by name, apparently—assured us that additional provisions would be smuggled in the following day.

Thanks to Zuri and Saleene, we'd hauled in our own supplies of lantern oil, water, blankets, and a bit of food. Iovis had made a token attempt at diverting food and bedding to Kaeto in a nod to his imperial status. Surprising me once again, Kaeto had not only flatly refused it, but had directed our provisions to be added to the general stockpile and handed out based on need.

The leaders ensured that the elderly and the very young had what they needed, and doled out the rest as best they could. The practical upshot was that Orlene, Val, Kaeto and I were down to two cloaks between us. That, along with the clothes we stood up in, were the only useful items we had.

Well… other than the coin purses Val, Orlene, and I carried—which didn't exactly meet the definition of usefulness in our current circumstances. Kaeto didn't even have that much to his name. Emperors didn't carry coin pouches on their person, as that would be far too vulgar for such an elevated ruler. Since he hadn't had money when I kidnapped—er, *rescued*—him in the gorge, it meant he didn't have money now.

There was nothing for us to do until morning, except hide down here among the bones of the dead. And it was bloody *cold.*

"Cold as the grave," Saleene muttered.

I thought wistfully of Eburos, where funerals meant raging pyres throwing sparks into the sky as the soul of the departed ascended to rejoin the ancestors in the gods' realm. I wandered restlessly around the echoing space, chafing my upper arms with my hands. I was relieved to see that Orlene had consented to huddle with Val beneath one of the cloaks, at least.

After the brothel, I hadn't been sure she would allow even *his* touch. I didn't pretend to understand what Orlene had gone through during her years as a prisoner of the Alyrion army. It had happened before I'd even been born, some thirty years ago when she was barely an adolescent.

Constanzus, Kaeto's father, had still harbored ambitions of conquering Eburos at the time. Orlene had been captured from her seaside village during a raid, and held for more than two years before being returned as part of a prisoner exchange. It didn't take unusual intelligence to guess what the soldiers had used her for... or why she wouldn't wish to impersonate a prostitute with Alyrion guardsmen breaking down doors to search the brothel.

To my knowledge, she'd only ever coupled with other women since her captivity. She and I had shared a few drunken fumbles a year or so ago, but any fool could see we were better matched as comrades than lovers. Orlene was a mass of jagged, razor-sharp edges, and I was emotionally defective in some way that made the language of romance feel as indecipherable and strange to me as rapidly spoken Kulawi.

Case in point—I'd managed to bed, and subsequently repel, both Orlene *and* Valeph since the two of them had joined the ranks of Eburosi dragonriders. Neither of them appeared to harbor any resentment about it, but it still made for a vaguely awkward command structure.

Anyway, I was glad that Orlene hadn't closed herself off completely. It helped that Val was a eunuch, and one of the least threatening people I knew—at least until he started tossing daggers or lit firepowder bombs around.

They would keep each other warm.

I rubbed my arms harder, unable to suppress a full-body shiver as I wandered along a wall made of skulls embedded in a hexagonal, honeycomb structure of... arm bones? I was pretty sure they were arm bones.

"Would you stop pacing and *sit down*?" Kaeto's rusty-voiced grumble startled me from my perusal of the mortared condyles. "You're making me twitchy."

"I'm cold," I told him, pitching my voice low enough to hopefully not bother the other people dozing on the floor around the edges of the vault. "I need to keep moving."

His eyes and the gaunt hollows beneath his cheekbones were dark shadows in the flickering light of the oil lamps. We stared at each other for long moments, then he grudgingly raised an arm, lifting the cloak he was huddled under.

I continued to stare, because… *what?*

His eyebrows dipped in a thunderous scowl. "Stop gawping, woman. Do I have to make it an imperial decree? You went to enough trouble to insinuate yourself into a position as my servant, did you not? Well, it seems I have need of your body heat tonight. *Attend me.*"

My muscles remained frozen for the space of several heartbeats before physical discomfort overrode good sense. With a huff, I turned and settled myself next to him on the stone floor, ducking beneath his outstretched arm. My body slotted against his side with more ease than it should have.

He hesitated for a brief instant before wrapping his arm—and the cloak—around my shoulders. Despite the impressive height and breadth of Orlene, the cloak's owner, it wasn't quite large enough to envelop both of us fully. Even so, it insulated us from the cold stone we were sitting on and the cold bones at our back.

I wriggled around a bit until I was able to draw the edge partway over my legs and torso. Combined with the heat radiating from Kaeto's body, within a few moments, I was nearly comfortable. My aching muscles began to unknot almost despite myself.

"I'm surprised at your reticence, after that performance in the whores' establishment," Kaeto muttered.

I shot him a sidelong glance. "I thought we were never speaking of that again."

There was a pause.

"Quite right," he said. "My mistake."

"Considering the fact that up until a couple of days ago, you might reasonably have wanted to stick a knife in me given the opportunity, I'm not sure my *reticence* should be all that surprising," I told him, still keeping my voice low.

His only response was a wordless noise of acknowledgement.

I tried not to succumb to the exhaustion tugging at my body and mind now that we were safe. It had been too long since I'd rested against another warm body, secure in someone else's embrace. Since before I came to Alyrios, certainly.

You like him, sing-songed a familiar mental voice.

He's an arsehole, I thought grumpily.

You're an arsehole, too, Xael pointed out, an observation that wasn't completely without merit. *So, that means you match, right?*

Fuck off, I told him.

It wasn't exactly a witty and devastating riposte, but my body was already sliding into sleep as the last few days finally caught up with me.

TWENTY-FOUR

It took three full days for the pagans to organize our escape via freight barge. At least, that's how long they told us it had been—the unchanging shadows inside the underground vaults made it impossible to keep track of time in any meaningful way.

Our supplies were smuggled in at intervals by grubby children clad in rags. Street orphans, I was guessing—their small, underfed forms both omnipresent and invisible in a city as large as Amarius. Children laboring under heavy burlap sacks filled with miscellaneous goods would be such a common sight that any guards sent out by Bruccias wouldn't even notice them.

When the woman with the brother who hauled freight finally returned, it was a massive relief. As appreciative as I was of the safe haven offered by the catacombs, the eerie surroundings were starting to make me feel decidedly strange in the head.

Stranger than usual? Xael teased.

You're one to talk, I sent back churlishly.

"We'll have to smuggle you down to the river dock in one of the freight wagons," the woman told us. "Then they can load you onto the barge with the rest of the cargo."

Our go-between was pale and thin, with lank brown hair and worry lines at the corners of her mouth. I still didn't know her name, and I got the impression she preferred it that way.

"What kind of cargo are we talking about, here?" Orlene asked warily.

"Cowhides," the woman said. "They stink before tanning, so no one will want to inspect them too closely."

"Lovely," Orlene muttered.

The woman gave a sheepish shrug. "It was either that or salted fish."

"Yeah, we'll take the cowhides, thanks," I said, before any of the others could protest. I wondered why Kaeto wasn't making more of a fuss about this new development, but then I realized he'd probably never smelled an untanned cowhide in his privileged imperial life.

"When do we leave?" the emperor asked.

"Two hours before sunrise, Your Majesty," said the woman, dipping her head in a shallow bow. "We're to meet the wagons in an alley behind the city abattoir. The catacombs will take us most of the way there."

❧◈❧

We must have traversed more than two miles of twisting underground tunnels by lantern light, when our guide finally called a halt at the base of a rickety wooden staircase leading up to street level. "This is it. We can get the rest of the way to the alley by moving between buildings."

Saleene and Zuri had accompanied us on the journey beneath the city, along with the man and woman who seemed to lead the group sheltering in the catacombs. I turned to the brothel owners, frowning in concern.

"You could come with us," I said. "Get out of Amarius."

"*No*," Kaeto and Saleene said in perfect unison. On this matter, at least, it appeared they were in accord.

Zuri sighed. "We'll stay. Saleene doesn't thrive in rural settings. Besides, we have a brothel to run."

"You're certain?" I asked.

"Very," Saleene said in a tone of finality.

I nodded. "In that case, thank you for everything."

Saleene snorted. "Don't mention it. In return, you can pay me back by never darkening my doorway again." Her sour gaze raked over Kaeto. "That goes double for you, *Your Imperial Majesty*."

"I'd rather spend an eternity packed in the salted fish we've so narrowly avoided," Kaeto replied.

"Tell Caius we said hello, the next time you see him," Zuri told me, ignoring the sniping.

Kaeto gave her a sharp look, which he then transferred to me.

"If we cross paths again, I will," I demurred, since the subject of Caius was still a sensitive one.

Farewells completed, we made our way up the creaking steps, following the freight master's sister into the stinking darkness outside. I'd never been to this part of Amarius before—not a surprise, since very few people voluntarily visited an abattoir unless they had unavoidable business there. Behind me, I heard Kaeto retch as the stench hit him.

Slipping through the narrow spaces between buildings, we eventually came upon the promised alley, and in it, the promised goods wagon. Money changed hands between the woman and the driver. Shortly thereafter, we were bundled into the back, where large crates packed with stiff, hairy hides took up all the available space.

With a bit of grunting and a lot of cursing, the four of us were manhandled into four of the crates that only held a few hides instead of dozens apiece. The woman helped us arrange the decoy hides around and on top of our bodies, hiding us from view through the slats. The sound of a hammer echoed loudly around the alley as lids were nailed on, trapping us inside.

It was every bit as uncomfortable and nauseating as it sounded, made worse as the wagon rattled over rough and rutted roads.

I may never eat beef again, I thought, when we finally rolled to a stop some considerable time later.

It doesn't stink if you sear it right away, said my oh-so-helpful fire breathing companion. *Serves humans right for letting the hides sit around so long.*

Thanks for the tip, I told him, not sparing the sarcasm.

Dockworkers' voices called back and forth outside the muffled confines of my crate. The wagon springs shifted as unloading began, until finally my stinky little world shifted and swayed dizzily around me.

"Check that freight for contraband," someone called from close by. "The guards have been riding my arse all week about regulations."

I held my breath, which helped surprisingly little when it came to the stink. The creak and splinter of a pry bar being applied to a nearby crate filtered through to my ears. It was in fate's hands now; if they'd chosen one of the others' hiding places to open, we were royally screwed.

I might or might not be able to wriggle onto my back and kick the lid of my own crate free, but there was absolutely no way to get out of my wooden prison stealthily if one of my companions was discovered.

An agonizingly long time passed before the muffled voice said, "This looks fine. Let 'em go through."

The tension flowed out of my shoulders. More scuffling and rustling, and my crate swayed again as I was lifted and loaded onto—I hoped—the barge. The whole thing seemed to take a small eternity, before the queasy, sideways feeling of a water-going vessel casting off and getting underway made my insides shift unpleasantly.

More time passed, and someone knocked on the slats of my crate. "We're outside the city," said a male voice. "I'm letting you out now."

When the lid of my crate finally fell away, I half-climbed and half-fell out of the mess of cowhide on limbs that had gone numb and tingly from confinement.

"Oh, thank the gods," I groaned, collapsing onto my back on the wooden deck. A few feet away, Val sat propped against the side of his open crate, looking as disgruntled and peeved as a pampered white cat who'd been tossed into a mud puddle.

I looked around the strange vessel as the man who'd freed me moved onto the next crate. The barge wasn't much more than a giant raft with a rudder on one end, packed with boxes, bags, and crates. Four posts set at the corners of the craft held lanterns aloft, illuminating wavering circles of orange light in the murky predawn darkness.

Half a dozen strong men stood at intervals along the stern, pushing the barge upstream through the sluggish river with long poles wielded in eerie unison.

The sound of gagging drew my attention back to my companions. It was Kaeto, free of his crate — but not, it appeared, of his delicate stomach. Orlene was the last to emerge, grim-faced and silent in the flickering light.

"There you go," said our savior. "I don't have much to offer, but I'll get you some dried rations and watered wine."

"Brilliant," I said, just as Kaeto started retching again.

❧ ♛ ☙

We managed to catch perhaps an hour of sleep before dawn brought its onslaught of biting insects. This, of course, was the reason that few people traveled by river during the summer season.

The stoic barge captain showed us how to don the gauzy, robe-like coverings he provided us. The hoods could be pulled all the way over the wearer's head and tucked into the neckline, turning the world into a hazy, unfocused dreamscape beyond the loosely woven fabric.

The sleeves were gathered at the wrist and tied with lengths of twine, leaving the excess fabric to fall over our hands. All in all, it was an incredibly inconvenient and cumbersome garment… one that was still considerably better than being covered in hundreds of bites and contracting swamp fever.

We rested as best we could in the humid heat of the day, swatting and scratching at the occasional ambitious bug that managed to infiltrate the gauzy robes.

"You could call the dragons here," Kaeto said in a low voice, as the bloated orange sun sank ponderously below the horizon. "There is no need to stay on this wreck of a barge being eaten by midges for two more days."

I couldn't see Orlene and Val's faces well enough to make out their reactions through their hoods, but I'd suspected this would be coming.

"No," I told him, my tone unyielding. "I won't bring our dragons into this conflict. Not without a formal treaty in place—one that I'm not qualified to negotiate, and you aren't currently in a position to uphold."

I'd given this a lot of thought over the past few days. The temptation to swoop into Heleva with the emperor on dragonback and declare his intent to overthrow his usurping younger brother with fiery retribution from the skies was undeniable. But the number of ways it could go horrifically wrong was staggering.

The leaders of Eburos hadn't sent us here to get involved in a civil war.

Kaeto grunted, displeased with my argument but evidently unable to counter it—for now, at least. He knew better than most how valuable a weapon the dragons were. If he'd been on the other side of this discussion, and I'd asked him for a similar boon with no expectation of commensurate reward, he'd have laughed in my face.

And so, we continued our miserable journey down the river, sleeping as much of the day away as we could, and eating unappealing dried rations at night. The journey was a more direct route than the path through the mountains, at least. While poling upstream against the sluggish current of the Uvi was by no means fast travel, it was no slower than traveling with a pack train of mules.

On the third night, only a few hours after the sun set, the lights of Heleva came into view as we rounded a bend in the waterway. My relief at the imminent end of our journey, gave way to new tension when the captain called, "Something's wrong!"

I joined the others at the front of the vessel— peering ahead into the darkness, unable to make sense of what I was seeing. In the distance, a string of lights stretched across the width of the river like a glowing necklace.

"What *is* that?" Kaeto demanded.

"I don't know," replied the captain, sounding grim. "You four, get out of sight. Hide in the back with the crates."

Misgivings ate at my stomach like vitriol, but I nodded sharply and herded the others toward the confusion of cargo containers near the stern. We jammed ourselves into the spaces between rows of crates as best we could, falling silent except for our rapid breathing.

The barge sculled onward, until a harsh voice cut through the night air.

"Halt! On the orders of Emperor Bruccias, the city of Heleva is under blockade! All traffic in and out is to be detained and searched. Approach the line of ships and moor to the nearest in preparation for boarding!"

TWENTY-FIVE

I cursed softly and fluently under my breath, damning Bruccias, Kaeto, and the entire benighted imperial bloodline to their god's fiery realm of punishment.

"We can't risk being discovered and captured," Val whispered, his tone urgent.

Orlene's green eyes bored into me in the lamplight. *Make a decision before the troops blockading the river make it for you,* that gaze said.

"Fuck," I snapped, and turned to Kaeto. "*Please* tell me you can swim."

"Of course I can swim," Kaeto snapped back. "Heleva is on the right bank of the river. Come on—there's no time to waste."

"Unbuckle your weapons belts, all of you," I said. "Try to hold onto them, but if it's a choice between ditching your blades and drowning, let the river have them."

I suited action to word, well aware of the perils of trying to cross a river while weighed down by clothing, boots, and steel blades. Leading the way, I crept to the back of the barge and slipped into the water. Three more quiet splashes reached my ears as the others followed suit.

The water was cold but not frigid. This close to Heleva, it stank of an entire city's worth of sewage.

I hoped the others knew better than to swallow any of it if they could possibly avoid it.

In short, the next little while was going to be exceptionally unpleasant.

Taking a deep breath, I let go of my one-handed grip on the barge's deck and kicked off toward the right bank, using an awkward sidestroke to accommodate the sword belt slung over my opposite shoulder.

In no time at all, the edge of the barge's pool of lantern light slipped away, leaving me in disorienting darkness. At first, swimming wasn't too difficult, but it became harder and harder as the water permeated my clothing, making everything heavy.

There was absolutely no way to keep track of the others while still making forward progress. In the absence of anyone crying out for help, the only clue I had that they were nearby was the soft, directionless sound of splashing.

I was determined not to lose my godsdamned sword, but the amount of effort directed toward keeping my head above the surface as opposed to swimming actively toward the bank was becoming alarming.

Were the others keeping up? I wanted to call out, demand a head count... but what if we were within earshot of the troops stationed across the waterway?

They could swim. I *knew* they could swim. Maybe I should worry more about myself and less about them.

The bank was a lighter smear of sandy brown in the distance, illuminated by starlight. I could make out the darker silhouette of trees beyond it, blotting out the night sky behind them. Were we getting any closer? Naloth's *balls*, it sure didn't bloody feel like it.

As exhaustion began to drag at my muscles, Xael's unobtrusive presence nudged further into my consciousness, his worry prickling at my thoughts.

I'm fucking fine, I sent, through the mental equivalent of gritted teeth. *Never better. Seriously, I live for this kind of shit.*

I couldn't spare the concentration to wonder about what Xael was doing when he abruptly pulled back from the link. Not beyond thinking that it was usually a lot harder than that to offend him.

Ugh. Was the riverbank any closer *at all*?

A louder splash came from somewhere behind me and to my left, followed by a gasping cough. Adrenaline shot through me, lending my muscles strength as I wallowed around in the water until I was facing in the direction the noise had come from.

At first, there didn't seem to be anything to see. The water was dark, the sky was dark, everything was fucking *dark*. Then a pale head emerged, spluttering, only to disappear again.

"Val!" I gasped, flailing toward the place where he'd been. I was too far away—we'd drifted apart as we swam, and my body was so heavy that it felt like I was pushing through treacle.

I dropped my sword belt without a second thought, the blade sinking into the depths, lost forever. Panic thrummed through my heaving chest. *Why wasn't Val surfacing again?*

I struggled toward the undifferentiated stretch of black water, caught up in the nightmarish sensation of making no progress even though the situation was life and death. Ahead of me, fresh splashing erupted. I strained to see what was happening, but my field of vision was nothing more than a churn of dark waves.

I was still a good twenty feet away when the churning erupted upward, revealing two heads—one dark, one pale. Val descended into a paroxysm of coughing and gagging, while the dark figure snarled, "Come on, damn you! Lie back and kick your legs—it's not that far!"

Kaeto.

He'd dragged Val back to the surface and was pulling him toward the indistinct outline of the shore. I struggled to shove down my panic over what had nearly happened and struck out after them. It was easier now that I wasn't hauling my sword belt with me, even though the loss of my weapons constituted an entirely separate reason to panic.

The remainder of the distance felt endless, but I kept Kaeto and Val's heads firmly in my line of sight and used their presence as an anchor. From somewhere ahead, a familiar voice called, "This way! There's a sandbar!"

I recognized Orlene with a flood of relief, and nearly shouted in jubilation when my hands and knees unexpectedly touched bottom. In front of me, Kaeto and Val staggered upright, leaning against each other in the knee-deep water. I crawled up the sandbar to where they were waiting, not trusting my legs to support me unaided as the three of us joined Orlene on dry land.

Kaeto let Val go. The former priest immediately collapsed to his knees, leaning over and heaving up what looked like half the river. Kaeto stayed on his feet, bent at the waist and bracing his hands on his thighs as he panted.

Orlene hurried to Val's side. I staggered over to join them.

"What happened?" Orlene demanded. "*Godsdamn* it, I didn't even hear anything!"

"He was trying to keep one of those demonic fire pouches of his dry," Kaeto panted, straightening up and slicking his soaked hair back from his face. "And that long tunic of his wasn't bloody well helping matters, either."

"You saved him," I said stupidly, my hand wrapped around Val's arm as he shuddered and coughed. Orlene looked at me sharply, then back at Kaeto.

"Saved *him*," Kaeto echoed sourly, "and lost all our weapons in the process. Not to mention making enough of a commotion to attract the troops' attention if any of them happened to be looking our way. Did you two manage to keep your swords?"

"No," I replied, not feeling remotely happy about the fact.

"Yes," Orlene said tersely, taking Val by the shoulders and supporting him as he doubled over and started heaving again.

"We need to get under cover," I said. "I saw trees earlier."

I tried to rise and stumbled. A cold hand closed around my bicep before I could go down in an ignominious heap, steadying me on my feet. Tracing the attached arm to its owner, I found Kaeto scowling at me in the weak starlight. Val groaned softly as Orlene hauled him upright, slinging his arm over her broad shoulders.

"This is bad," Kaeto murmured in my ear, too low for the others to hear. "We have no dry clothes, no cloaks or blankets, and only one of us is armed. Even if we could somehow start a fire for warmth, doing so would serve as a beacon for my brother's troops to find us."

"I'm painfully aware," I replied. "For now, getting to the trees is our best bet. We don't know yet how badly Val fared, and whether he'll be able to travel." I paused, gazing up at the dark shadows obscuring Kaeto's gray eyes. "Thank you for rescuing him. I wouldn't have reached him in time, and even if I had, I might not have been strong enough to tow him to the riverbank."

Kaeto was silent for a moment. "He facilitated our escape from the palace guards in Amarius," he said eventually. "I was merely repaying the debt."

Right.

"Of course you were," I replied. Testing my legs gingerly, I took a couple of steps without falling and nodded to show I was all right to walk. Kaeto released my arm.

I eyed the sandy slope leading up to the tree line. "Let's go," I told the others.

Shivering, the four of us made our slow way toward the promise of shelter—if not from the night's chill, then hopefully from the prying eyes of any troops sent to flush us out.

TWENTY-SIX

Valeph was not in good shape. I was worried that he'd inhaled the foul water from the river as well as swallowing it, and if so, we were in trouble if we couldn't get him somewhere with a good healer.

Downstream as we were from the port town of Heleva, the Uvi was tainted with the residents' waste. He was almost certainly going to have an intestinal illness, but pneumonia could kill him even faster.

Unfortunately, right now the only way we were likely to get inside Heleva's walls was if we were hauled there in chains after being captured by Bruccias' siege forces. Even now, mercenary soldiers were crashing through the trees to our south, searching for us. And Val's uncontrollable coughing fits as his body tried to expel the water he'd taken in weren't exactly helping our chances.

"Keep moving," I whispered, supporting Val from one side as Orlene supported him from the other.

The forest that bordered the river was dense with old-growth trees, but it wasn't so thick with underbrush that it offered a plethora of good hiding places. I was trying to decide if there was any conceivable way for us to shin up one of the larger trees and hide among the branches when Orlene caught my eye over Val's shoulder.

"Panosh is being awfully quiet," Orlene said in a low voice. "It's starting to worry me."

I frowned. Orlene's copper-colored dragon wasn't usually what you'd call *circumspect*.

"Rensa, too," Val wheezed, leaning heavily against me as he stumbled over a root.

"Xael as well," I said, steadying myself with the thick tree branch I'd managed to break off to use as a quarterstaff. "He pulled back from the bond when we were in the river."

Kaeto, currently taking point with Orlene's sword in hand, glanced over his shoulder at us in the uncertain predawn grayness. "What does that mean, exactly?"

I sighed, not sure whether to be relieved or pissed off as the obvious answer presented itself. "It means they're probably flying here as we speak."

Kaeto came to a halt and turned to face us. "You called for them?"

"Nope," I told him grimly. "At a guess, they thought we were going to die and decided they needed to come save us. And now they're pretending they can't hear us so we can't tell them not to."

"Think they might... have a point," Val croaked weakly.

"He's not wrong," Orlene said.

Kaeto stilled as distant shouting came from somewhere to our left, closer to the river. He met my eyes and lowered his voice.

"Perhaps you will rethink your unwillingness to involve the beasts," he said. "You've just admitted that you can't call them off, and frankly I'm skeptical of the likelihood of your friend's survival if we're left to our own devices."

He didn't add that the odds for the rest of us weren't looking so great, either. He didn't have to.

"We could break the blockade on the port," Orlene said quietly. She jerked her chin toward Kaeto. "Get that one inside the city walls with his loyal troops. He's still our best chance to get the eggs back, especially if Bruccias has them."

The idea that Bruccias might have dragons was a nightmare scenario, and I knew it. Even so, using our own dragons to crush an Alyrion fighting force wasn't remotely within the scope of our mission. If the dragons were coming—and I had no doubt they were—there was another option.

We could fly Kaeto to safety, across the border with Utrea, and he could try to negotiate his own damned treaty with King Rathanii.

Beside me, Val tried to suppress another coughing fit. He wouldn't be able to manage a flight that long, I realized with a jolt. He was near collapse as it was.

This decision was on me. Orlene and Val would support it, no question. I wasn't sure about Kaeto—but in the end, it wasn't their opinions that mattered. It was *my* mission, and *my* responsibility.

Even if it meant dragging my people into a war.

"I'll consider it," I said. "Come on. We need to keep moving."

Kaeto nodded cautiously and turned to continue our wending way through the forest.

I was distracted with trying to calculate how long it would take the dragons to fly here from their hiding place in the mountains to the west, when the trees ahead of us opened into a decent-sized grassy clearing. Kaeto came to a halt so abrupt that the rest of us nearly plowed into his back.

"Problem," he said, in an unnaturally calm voice.

From across the clearing came a startled shout. "There they are!" cried a deep voice. "Capture them!"

"Well, *fuck*," Val rasped, uncharacteristically profane.

I dropped his arm, grasping my pathetic quarterstaff in both hands. "Orlene—get him under cover in the trees," I snapped. "We'll hold them off!"

Orlene growled something under her breath, but I was already rushing forward to stand shoulder to shoulder with Kaeto. He shot me a sidelong glance as four mercenaries charged into the clearing opposite us.

"I can't help noting that Orlene might have been the better choice of defender," he said. "She's twice your size."

"She's also shit with a quarterstaff," I retorted.

Whereas I was a shivering, exhausted wreck after my unplanned swim, while Kaeto was once more limping on his bad knee after overexerting himself during this latest little adventure.

It was just possible that my judgment wasn't currently at its best.

"Right," he said, raising Orlene's sword in a two-handed grip as our opponents barreled toward us.

I barely had time to set myself next to him before two men were upon me. The bark of the unpeeled tree branch tore at the skin of my hands as I rammed one end of the makeshift staff into the first man's gut, then smoothly swung the other end around to land a glancing blow against the second one's helmet.

A pained grunt came from somewhere to my right as Kaeto clashed with the other two. I couldn't spare enough attention to check on him, because the second soldier was already coming at me again, more cautiously this time.

Behind him, his companion groaned and started climbing to his feet. I itched with the need to put him down for good, but he was going to be back in the fight before long. The man I'd failed to knock out with a head blow feinted left and swung his sword low, aiming for a knee or hamstring slice. I parried it sharply. The staff was nearly jerked out of my grip when his blade cut into the soft bark and stuck there for a moment.

Deresta's *tits*—if he hit much harder, he'd end up slicing my makeshift weapon in half.

The rapid clang of steel against steel rang out from a few strides away, interspersed with more grunts and the occasional cry of pain. I gave ground, needing to draw my opponent back far enough that I could keep an eye on Kaeto...

knowing in the pit of my stomach that we were both incredibly fucked at this point.

The downed soldier heaved himself to his feet, clutching his stomach for a moment before straightening and stalking toward me as well, his sword still in hand.

I swung out with the staff, driving the soldier closest to me back half a step. Gods, what I wouldn't give for a couple of the throwing knives that were now decorating the bottom of the riverbed.

In my peripheral vision, the two men attacking Kaeto charged him in unison, and he went down with a cry. Heart hammering, I shouted something wordless and lunged toward him, staff raised. A crashing blow from one of my opponents sent it spinning out of my grip, ripping skin off my palms as it did so.

Weaponless, I ducked a second strike that would have taken my head off, my sore body protesting as I hit the ground and rolled. I landed on my back, staring up at the angry face and raised sword of the man I'd hit in the gut.

Well, this is an embarrassing way to go, I thought, as the man's lips curled into a sneer. *Sorry, Xael.*

As though my thoughts had summoned him, an ear-splitting shriek echoed from above. The man standing over me looked up at the sky, his mouth gaping open. A burst of flame about twenty paces to my left illuminated the clearing with shifting orange light, and the man screamed in terror.

Forcing my aching muscles into compliance, I curled my legs up and kicked out, shoving him backward onto his arse. Another gout of flame from above ignited the grass on the far side of the clearing.

Scrambling to my feet, I staggered forward and stepped on the nearest man's wrist, reaching down to wrench his sword from his weakened grasp. He cowered, his eyes darting between me and the dawn sky above… his mouth gaping in shock. I sliced the blade across his throat, stepping back as he convulsed, blood spurting.

Looking around through the smoke and confusion, I found my other opponent gone. Fled into the trees, presumably.

One of Kaeto's opponents lay unmoving on the ground. The other one was running away, favoring one leg heavily. Kaeto was upright, but even as I stumbled toward him, he swayed and fell to his knees.

"Darra!" Orlene's shout was nearly lost beneath the crackle of fire and the ringing in my ears. I peered through watering eyes, just able to make out the blurry forms of her and Val entering the clearing.

A strong downdraft whipped up the flames consuming the grass a short distance away from us, and a moment later, a massive form thumped down nearby.

Shouldn't have left us behind in the mountains, Xael's voice rumbled inside my head. *Boats are stupid. Now you're all wet and cold. Rensa was frightened.*

No more boats, I agreed silently, as two more large forms came in for an ungainly landing in the cramped confines of the clearing. *We'll have to have a talk about disobeying orders... but I'm really glad you're here.*

TWENTY-SEVEN

Three dragons, four humans, and two slowly cooling corpses in one medium-sized clearing—which also happened to be *very slightly on fire*—made for an uncomfortable squeeze.

Xael politely folded his wings away, while Rensa, Val's little white female, charged past us to reach her rider. Xael had said she was frightened. I suspected that was an understatement. Val had nearly drowned, and if Kaeto hadn't dragged him out of the river, Rensa would have perished right along with him when their bond broke.

"We need to get away from here," Kaeto called, over the happy screeching and chittering as Panosh and Rensa reunited with Orlene and Val. "With these fires blazing, we'll have an army descending on us before long."

I crossed to him and reached down, grabbing his sleeve to help pull him to his feet. The fabric was still wet and cold with river water. A fresh bruise decorated his jaw. We braced each other on our feet—two exhausted and battered people whose options were narrowing down to a single, clear road forward.

"We're going to break the siege," I told him. "You'll have to ride Xael. I'm the lightest—I'll ride double with Val and keep him from falling off Rensa."

Kaeto stilled. "The last time I graced that beast's back, he nearly broke my neck."

My lips pulled back into something that wasn't quite a smile. "Then you'd better not piss him off this time."

He stared at me for a long moment in the flickering red-orange light. Then his mask fell smoothly back into place. "Easy enough," he said. "Well, then… if we're finally agreed that mayhem is the next item on the agenda, what are we waiting for?"

I gave a sharp nod and turned to inform the others.

A wryly amused presence threaded through my thoughts. *I suppose that means I can't eat him?*

He'd only give you indigestion, I sent back.

"Time to leave," I called to our companions. "We've got a mercenary army to burn. Val, you're with me on Rensa. Xael can carry Kaeto."

Orlene lifted her chin, one hand resting on Panosh's scaly shoulder. "So, we're really doing this, huh?"

"We are," I agreed. "We've got at least one influential ally in the city, assuming nothing happened to him while I was gone. We'll get Kaeto to safety and Val to a healer. Everything else can wait."

"You don't need to tell me twice," Orlene said.

Panosh bowed low, stretching his front end down to rest on his good leg. Where his right front leg should have been, there was only a short stump—a defect he'd had upon hatching, despite being otherwise healthy.

Orlene grasped one of the bony spikes growing from his back and stepped up on the crook of his wing, swinging herself into position in the dip behind the base of his mighty neck.

I craned around to see Xael eyeing Kaeto with a beady amethyst gaze as the deposed emperor contemplated how best to haul his battered body onto the dragon's back. He was halfway through a comically undignified scramble when Xael twisted his head around and gave him a helpful shove in the seat of his breeches, nearly overbalancing him.

Kaeto cursed sharply and grabbed for the nearest handhold, righting himself before he could topple off the other side. Val muttered something I didn't catch, and promptly descended into a coughing fit. I stepped close and wrapped an arm around his slender frame, supporting him.

"Little help here, Rensa," I told the sleek white female. "Val—shift your arse."

"Thought shifting was... more your department," Val wheezed.

"More my father's department, you mean," I said sourly, sparing a thought for my lion-shifter sire. "Up you get."

Between Rensa's careful nudging and my less careful shoving, we managed to get Val aboard. I climbed up after him, wondering who I was going to have to bribe to get a week of uninterrupted sleep in a nice, comfortable bed somewhere.

Rensa was the smallest of our three dragons, and she wouldn't normally have been the best candidate for riding double. But she was Val's, and their bond made her the most logical choice to carry him. She wouldn't jostle him more than necessary, and she'd be able to tell if his balance started to go.

Between us, we'd keep him from falling off.

Watch out for civilian barges or captured transport ships, but any troops blocking access to the town are fair game, I told Xael. *Lead the way.*

With an excited screech, Xael spread his wings and pushed off, Kaeto clinging grimly to his neck spikes as the dragon launched himself into the smoky air. Panosh followed, with the ungainly double flap he always used to compensate for his missing front leg.

When they were safely aloft, I wrapped a steadying arm around Val and grasped for a good handhold.

"Hang on tight," Val rasped. "This clearing isn't very big."

I gripped with my knees as Rensa reared back and charged across the glade of burning grass, taking a run-up to get more lift beneath our combined weight. Pearly wings stretched wide, the little dragon's muscles bunching and releasing beneath my legs as she flapped hard, catching the breeze.

I held my breath as we lifted into the air, the trees at the edge of the clearing approaching too close and too fast. Rensa kicked out, her hind legs scrabbling against branches as we grazed the treetops.

Another flap, and we were clear. The wind grew chilly against my damp clothing as we gained altitude, and I knew Val wouldn't be faring any better on that front. I pressed my chest to his back, hoping to transmit my body heat to him.

He shivered in my arms, his chest hitching as he fought not to cough. Rensa gave an unhappy bleat at whatever she was sensing through the bond, but she flew after the others straight and true. Above the shadow of the trees and the plumes of smoke, the sun breached the horizon, half obscured by gray clouds.

There was a definite sense of surreality as the dragons got their bearings, banking toward the line of ships and floating buoys blocking the river. Xael and I had burned the occasional small military target over the years, and he'd helped me destroy the raider camp in the mountains to rescue Aelio and his men.

But Eburos was not at war with any other nations. It hadn't been during my lifetime. This was the first time its dragonriders had ever faced a foreign army—albeit a mercenary one. Words reached my ears past the wind, and I realized that Val was muttering a prayer for the dead. Ahead of us, Xael swooped low, flames shooting down to engulf the first of the blockade's ships.

Then the screaming started in earnest.

As Panosh and Rensa added their flames to the destruction, it was almost frightening how effortless the attack seemed. Bruccias' mercenary troops had no dragon harpoons with them—there was absolutely no reason why they *would*. Even the strongest archer couldn't shoot a normal arrow with enough force and distance to pierce the scales of dragons in flight. The soldiers below had no defense against us.

And that was the true power of dragons. It was why someone—most likely Bruccias—had thought it worthwhile to risk a war by stealing eggs. Without their own dragon army, not even a vast empire like Alyrios could stand against tiny, upstart nations like Eburos, much less more established dynasties like Utrea.

The mercenary troops numbered well over a thousand—more likely two or three thousand. They circled the walled town on all sides, their numbers concentrated around the roads and canals. Whole regiments broke and ran when they realized what was raining down on them from the sky.

Xael sent a question—*follow?*—but I called him back to finish the job of shattering the blockade. Right now, freeing the port and getting Kaeto and Val to safety was more important than massacring every fleeing soldier. Val's trembling had grown to full-body shudders as our flight continued, the wind sapping our combined body heat even as our clothes dried on our backs.

We circled the city three times, looking for stragglers or groups trying to shelter in the woods. Choking gray smoke billowed into the air in thick plumes. I sent a wordless apology to anyone in Heleva who relied on logging in the nearby forests for a livelihood. They were going to be traveling farther afield for their wares after the morning's carnage.

"We're going into the city," I shouted against the wind, sending the same message through my link with Xael. "Look for a military garrison!"

The dragons circled inward, flying over the port itself. The wind and smoke made my aching eyes water, but I scanned the ground below until a fortified wall surrounding a group of blocky buildings swam into view.

"That's it!" I cried, pointing with the arm that wasn't wrapped around Val.

We spiraled lower, more of the scene below us coming into focus. I blinked rapidly, straining to make out details. And... *there*. A sandy-haired figure stood on the highest rampart—leaning heavily against a thick staff as he, in turn, scanned the sky with one hand shading his eyes.

TWENTY-EIGHT

To say that the troops stationed at the garrison were *on edge* as our dragons landed in the central parade ground was putting it mildly. Dozens of soldiers clattered into the open area to surround us—many of them looking as though they'd been rousted abruptly from their bunks before being ordered to act as potential dragon fodder.

"Hold!" Kaeto bellowed, sliding down from Xael's back with careful, stiff movements. "Do you not recognize your emperor?"

Confused muttering erupted among the gathering crowd—but on the positive side, none of them started firing crossbows or charging at us with swords.

A slender youth, perhaps twelve or thirteen years old, came running onto the scene, pushing his way through the ranks to get to the front. His eyes widened as he took in the three dragons crouched in the center of the open square, but he cleared his throat manfully and shouted, "Tribuni Aelio commands that the dragon riders be made welcome and given anything they need! He says the siege on Heleva is broken!"

I was close enough to see the way Kaeto froze in place upon hearing Aelio's name, but there was no time to devote to interpreting the odd reaction.

In my arms, Val doubled over and began to cough as though he might hack up a lung.

Kaeto seemed to tear himself free of whatever had paralyzed him a moment before.

"We need a physic—the best in the city," he called. "Have fresh meat brought here for the dragons. Then send someone who can deliver a report on the blockade. I need to know when it started, who commanded the forces, and whether they made any demands of the city's governor."

"Yes, sir!" the young runner said, turning to hare off again.

It was a testament to how exhausted he must be that Kaeto didn't try to tear the boy a new arsehole for not correctly addressing him as royalty. Instead, he turned to the nearest troops.

"Where is Tribuni Aelio now?" he asked.

Evidently, he hadn't seen his palace commander standing on the ramparts as we flew in. Or perhaps he hadn't recognized him in the confusion.

A grizzled old veteran stepped forward, bowing cautiously. "The tribuni went up to the top of the wall when word of the dragon attack reached us, sir. I mean, *sire*." He cleared his throat awkwardly, but Kaeto waved away the lapse. "It, uh, may take him some time to make his way back down again, with his bad leg and all."

"You'd be surprised," came a clear, familiar voice from across the parade ground. "Let's just say that I am *highly* motivated at the moment."

The soldiers parted, clearing a path in the same area where the runner had been forced to shove his way through earlier. The disconcerted muttering among the crowd faded as Aelio hobbled forward. His clear gaze landed on Xael's distinctive form for only a moment before honing in on Kaeto.

Once more, the erstwhile emperor of Alyrios went completely still, staring statue-like at his trusted commander. Aelio closed the distance with surprising speed, leaning heavily on his staff. He stopped a few steps away and fell into a deep bow, his bad leg held awkwardly out to the side as he gripped the wooden walking stick with both hands to keep from toppling forward onto his face.

"Your Imperial Majesty," he breathed. "I hardly dared believe it was true."

The excited conversation among the soldiers started up again, louder than before.

"*Aelio.*" Kaeto's voice emerged choked. He cleared his throat and limped forward, reaching down to grasp the tribuni's arm. "Get up, man. Dear *god*, am I glad to see your face."

"The feeling is entirely mutual, sire," Aelio said, straightening. "I gather we have you to thank for saving the city?"

His incisive gaze swept over Orlene before falling on Val and me. I forced a smile and gave him a sheepish, one-handed wave, wondering for about the hundredth time how soon I'd be able to get horizontal and lose consciousness for the foreseeable future.

"Once the physic arrives, I will require a full report on everything that's happened," Kaeto said.

Aelio frowned, doubtless having catalogued the limp and the spreading purple bruise on Kaeto's jaw. "You're injured, sire."

"The physic isn't for me." Kaeto jerked his chin toward Val. "That one nearly drowned in the river. The pale one, I mean — not the troublesome one."

"I see," Aelio said, after a faint pause. "Perhaps you will also provide me with a full accounting of recent events, Your Majesty."

"Yes." Kaeto sounded suddenly as weary as I felt. "Once the immediate practicalities are dealt with, I suppose I'd better."

⚜

The meat for the dragons arrived a few minutes before the healer did. But within half an hour, Val had been whisked off for treatment, with me in tow to make sure he was cared for properly.

Orlene insisted on staying to look after the dragons, while Kaeto had disappeared somewhere with Aelio to exchange reports. I wasn't quite prepared to say we were *safe*, but there was no doubt that our circumstances had improved considerably compared to a few hours ago.

The lad who'd been acting as Aelio's runner showed up at the healer's rooms with a platter of meat, cheese, and bread, which I was currently devouring while listening to the unpleasant sound of Val coughing up a slurry of stale river water and phlegm.

The healer — or rather, the physic, as they preferred to be called here in Alyrios — had tutted and muttered to himself as he pressed an ear to different parts of Val's chest. When I'd pushed for answers, he'd eventually stated that Val was likely to get worse before he got better, but that he had a particular tincture of some kind of fungus I'd never heard of before; one that often worked wonders in these cases.

After administering his treatment and following it up with some kind of foul-smelling decoction meant to quiet Val's cough, Val fell fast asleep within minutes.

"Is that normal?" I asked, quashing an unbecoming flare of jealousy as Val snored loudly, dead to the world.

"Yes," the physic said with satisfaction. "Sedation is a secondary effect. The sleep will do him good."

The man shooed me away a short time later, firmly stating that he would keep watch over Val, and that he didn't need a second person falling asleep in his treatment room. The messenger boy, who'd been hovering silently just outside the doorway, took one look at me and led me to a room down the hall with a neatly made-up cot and a washstand.

"I should check on the dragons," I protested, trying to ignore the way the cot tugged my body toward it like a lodestone.

"Your other companion—the red-haired one—is still with them," said the lad. "She insisted on bunking down with the animals. I will inform her where to find you if she needs you for anything, ma'am."

I wavered for a moment before reaching inward.

Is everything all right, Xael? I asked, needing that final reassurance.

All is well, came the reply. *But you are making me sleepy.* The mental impression of a huge yawn followed, and with that, I was done for.

"Thank you," I told the boy. "That would be much appreciated."

He bowed and gave me a cheeky grin before leaving me to my beautiful, softly padded horizontal surface. I trudged into the room, considered trying to wash off the stench of the river for approximately the space of one heartbeat, then collapsed face-first onto the bed instead. The half-healed bruise on my temple throbbed unhappily, but it wasn't enough to prevent me falling asleep the moment my head came to rest on the pillow.

When I next regained consciousness, it was dark outside the room's small window. That window overlooked the parade ground, and light from the torches burning around the edges of the large square illuminated my surroundings well enough to prevent me stumbling into anything as I dragged myself out of the bed.

I found the stub of a tallow candle on the washstand, along with a flint striker. After I lit it, I discovered that someone had left another tray of food just inside the open door. It was some kind of lentil stew, along with a chunk of crusty bread and a flagon of weak ale.

I ate and drank, though the stew and the ale had both grown lukewarm while I slept. This time around, I used the chamberpot and availed myself of the ewer of water and the sponge in the room. It was a lost cause against the stink of the river permeating my clothes, and I knew it. Still, the water felt good on my face and neck, helping me to wake up.

Retracing the route to the physic's rooms, I knocked softly on the door. It could have been the middle of the night for all I knew, but the door opened a few moments later.

The gray-haired healer took one look at me and said, "Your friend is still resting. He woke an hour or so ago and was able to take some broth and bread. It is best if you don't disturb him. I will send word if there is any significant change."

I craned past him to see Val resting on his side. His complexion held a grayish cast, but he wasn't in any apparent distress.

"Thank you," I told the man. "I'll be with the dragons. Don't hesitate to call if you need someone to watch over him later."

The physic looked mildly amused, if anything. "That will not be necessary. My apprentice will arrive in a few hours to take over while I rest. That said, once the patient is awake for a longer period of time, I will send for you. I'm sure he'd appreciate a visit."

The polite phrasing clearly translated to 'please go away and let me do my job,' so I thanked him again and wandered outside to find Orlene and the dragons. Despite the many hours of sleep

I'd just had, my body seemed intent on reminding me with every step that it had undergone quite a bit of abuse recently.

On the far end of the parade ground, Xael was keeping watch while Rensa and Panosh dozed. He rumbled a greeting as I scratched his scaly neck, tipping his nose toward a nearby open doorway when I silently inquired after Orlene.

I poked my head inside to find what seemed to be a storage area of some sort. Orlene was seated on a folded blanket laid on the dirt floor, her back resting against a sturdy support post.

"Wondered when you'd be back," she greeted. "How's Val doing?"

"The healer seems satisfied with his progress so far," I said. "He's mostly been resting, though he ate and drank a bit earlier. Has Rensa been calm?"

The little white dragon would know better than anyone if Val was in distress, whether he was conscious or not.

Orlene nodded. "Panosh says she doesn't seem too worried."

A touch of relief loosened my shoulders. "Good. Look, you should go find a real bed and get some proper sleep. I'll take over here. Did someone tell you how to get to the room I've been using?"

"Yeah," she replied, stretching and clambering stiffly to her feet. "A bed does sound pretty good."

I gave her directions from my room to the healer's place, so she could check on Val later. She clapped me on the shoulder as she passed. Once she'd gone, I eyed the folded blanket with a sigh and sank down on it, letting my head fall back against the post.

Wake me if anything interesting happens, I told Xael, and let my eyes slip closed.

The rest of the night passed in restless dozing. Morning light filtered in through the door when Xael nudged me mentally.

Something interesting is happening.

There was no sense of alarm behind the message. I winced and stretched my back, my muscles protesting as I climbed carefully to my feet. A figure darkened the doorway. I blinked the grit out of my eyes.

"You," Kaeto said, his voice a bare growl.

Before I could muster some version of a confused '*Huh?*', he'd closed the distance between us and pressed my back against the post. His sword-callused hand came up, framing my jaw. A pulse of instinctive alarm raced through me, only to be buried under shock when his lips crashed into mine in a harsh, demanding kiss.

TWENTY-NINE

The rush as Kaeto's chapped lips pressed against mine chased away my early morning grogginess. His tongue explored the seam of my lips, demanding entrance, and my body responded before my brain did, parting to allow him inside.

I had no idea what had brought this on, and it was likely I'd end up regretting it if I didn't shut this insanity down before it went any further. Unfortunately, I also had a history of using sex as a distraction from my worries—and right now, the gods knew I had plenty of those.

I was not and had never been the kind of person who needed mushy feelings to be involved in a sexual tryst. On the contrary, those mushy feelings had always been a complete mystery to me… much to the confusion and chagrin of several of my partners over the years.

Kaeto was an arsehole, but he was a surprisingly attractive arsehole. I'd gained a modicum of respect for him over the span of our acquaintance, similar to the respect one gained for a deadly pit viper that occasionally aimed its fangs at your enemy instead of at you.

Additionally, the part of my brain that wasn't thoroughly distracted by the delicious slide of his tongue against mine noted that having Kaeto better disposed toward me on a personal level could be useful to our goals, now that we were aligned together against Bruccias.

He was also a surprisingly good kisser.

Conclusion—there wasn't much of a downside here, and after almost three months of enforced celibacy, I was in desperate need of a good, hard fuck. When Kaeto's sword-callused hands started tearing at my ill-fitting stolen clothing, I didn't protest. Instead, I returned the favor.

At some point, Kaeto had exchanged his torn and travel-stained imperial finery for a simple open-necked tunic and breeches. This was good, because while tearing each other's clothes off might sound appealing in theory, in reality it was far from the most efficient way for two people to get naked.

I'd managed to get his tunic off when I remembered the small matter of this storage room having no door. I sent a brief, silent request to Xael not to let anyone approach, my train of thought cutting off rather abruptly when Kaeto—who'd succeeded in getting my top half bare as well— leaned down to nip sharply at a nipple.

Xael sighed with the long-suffering air of a dragon whose bonded rider did this sort of thing on a semi-regular basis, and who still found the whole concept a bit tiresome. He grumbled some sort of unintelligible acquiescence and retreated from the bond.

Kaeto's lips closed around the nipple he'd been worrying with his teeth, and the deep, drawing sensation felt like it had a direct line to my sex. Finding that I wasn't much in the mood for foreplay, I grabbed a fistful of Kaeto's hair and tugged him away, earning myself a choked groan.

Kaeto's gray eyes were blown wide and dark. I shoved him back a step so I could get my too-large trousers and boots off. He stood there unmoving, his chest rising and falling rapidly as I straightened before him, now fully nude. If anything, he looked a bit lost. Taking matters into my own hands, I reached for the laces holding his breeches closed and untied them. Not wanting to dawdle, I pushed them down past his lean hips, then repeated the process with his linen smallclothes.

"I trust I've finally earned the right to handle your imperial cock, Your Majesty?" I asked dryly, giving the cock in question a firm stroke.

He growled and shoved me back against the support post again. I took a moment to be thankful that age had worn the wood to a smooth patina, because splinters weren't sexy no matter how horny you were.

"I can handle my cock just fine without your help, firebrand," he said.

Grasping the meat of my thighs, he hefted me up until I was pinned between his hips and the post. I yelped and wrapped my legs around him, my head thunking back against the ancient wood as my bodyweight pressed me down, impaling me on his hard length as I went. We were both panting when he bottomed out. His head fell forward until our foreheads pressed together.

The stretch as my body opened to accommodate his length was divine, and so was the pressure of my nub against his pubic bone. My aching muscles and half-healed bruises might as well have belonged to a completely different person as I wriggled my hips, trying to get the friction I needed.

Kaeto made a punched-out noise, his hips flexing in response. His fingers dug into my thighs and arse; my fingers dug into the taut muscles of his shoulders where I was gripping him for balance.

Remembering the scene at the brothel, I reached around with one hand and deliberately dragged my ragged fingernails down the rippling muscles of his back — hard enough to leave welts.

His cock surged inside me.

"You are a demon in the shape of a woman," he growled... and then he was pounding into me, his movements just shy of violence.

I cried out in approval, raking his back with my nails like a wild beast as every brutal stroke drove me higher, barreling toward my release. I was going to have new bruises — hand-shaped ones on my thighs, and post-shaped ones on my back.

The gods knew what Kaeto's back was going to look like by the time I was finished with it. None of it mattered, because my climax was upon me, rolling through me like a storm battering the cliffs of Eburos. I moaned and clenched, dizziness assailing me. Strong arms held me in place through the tempest.

Kaeto pulled out, guiding me down to stand on shaky legs. His grip and the post behind me were the only things keeping me upright as he pressed his straining erection against the soft skin of my stomach, rubbing his length against me with frantic movements until his seed erupted between us in hot, slick spurts.

His body shuddered against mine as he spent, his breath warm and unsteady against the top of my head. I wrapped my arms around him, wondering if the dampness I felt beneath my hands was sweat... or blood from my nails.

I wasn't sure who managed to get us from our mostly upright position down to a horizontal tangle on the folded blanket—now a rucked mess of woven wool on the floor. Possibly, it was a joint effort. Kaeto's breeches had fallen down almost to his knees. He didn't seem to possess the will to pull them up.

We lay there for a few minutes in a mutual silence that felt very... *complete*. Eventually, Kaeto rolled onto an elbow, looking down at me in the light streaming through the open doorway. Still, he didn't say anything. Rather, he seemed to be trying to see directly through my skull and into the soft gray matter within.

"So..." I began cautiously. "Please don't take this the wrong way, since that was some *truly exceptional* sex, Your Majesty. But... what brought this on, exactly?"

Kaeto continued to gaze down at me with the same intensely thoughtful furrow in his brow. For a long moment, I wasn't sure he'd answer at all.

"You saved Aelio," he said eventually.

I blinked up at him, trying to make the words fit into the conversation we were having. "Well...

yes? I told you I did. I even gave you his cloak pin as evidence."

The furrow deepened. "I assumed you were lying to keep me complacent. You could have retrieved that pin from his corpse."

I shimmied inelegantly into a sitting position, so my eyes would be level with his.

"Wait. You thought I was lying *all this time*?" I asked. "And you never said anything?"

He opened his mouth to reply, only to pause and shake his head. When he spoke, his tone was more hesitant than I'd ever heard it.

"When you suggested coming here to Heleva... I began to have hope. But I couldn't afford to indulge it. Perhaps..." He hesitated and licked his lips before continuing. "Perhaps it is different where you come from, with your pale magicians who can sniff out falsehoods. But I grew up in a world where lies, and the ability to tell them, were the currency of survival. I... thought I had become adept at sensing them in others. I thought I had sensed them in *you*."

My own features folded into a frown. "Okay... but I'm still stuck on the part where you just went along with it. You even cooperated, once we agreed to ally ourselves against Bruccias. Why do that if you thought I was manipulating you?"

One dark eyebrow rose. "I found it unlikely that a lone woman—even a woman with a dragon—would be able to successfully extract an injured prisoner from a force as large as the one that attacked us in the ravine. However, it would have been a simple matter for you to make good on one of your many threats to burn me to death. My options did appear to be somewhat limited. Even more so, after your comrades arrived."

I stared at him, picturing this entire ordeal from his perspective, perhaps for the first time.

"Aelio is very valuable to me," Kaeto said carefully. "He is perhaps the first person in my life who ever saw something more in me than the cruel, scheming princep I once was. To have him safely returned to me is both unexpected, and a blessing."

I thought about that for a beat.

"Aelio is an honorable man," I said. "Someone wise once told me that we become the people with whom we surround ourselves. If that's the case, then I'm doubly glad I was able to save him for you."

"Perhaps what your wise man said is true," Kaeto replied. "It would certainly explain much about my family's history."

I thought of Bruccias. Of Constanzus, the old emperor who'd attempted to invade my homeland, causing so much death and destruction. Of Kaeto's own actions as a younger man.

I nodded, hugging my bare knees to my chest. "Maybe so. Now, we just have to figure out how to make sure the empire's future doesn't repeat the same mistakes from its past."

"Indeed," Kaeto agreed.

THIRTY

I managed to drag my oversized tunic and trousers on again before falling abruptly and unceremoniously asleep—the combination of exhaustion and the aftermath of really good sex demanding their due.

It wasn't a surprise when Orlene rapped her knuckles sharply against the doorframe some number of hours later, waking me from a sound slumber. It *was* a surprise to find Kaeto sitting propped against a barrel nearby, fully dressed and apparently having been watching me as I slept.

I wasn't the only one to be startled.

"Darra," Orlene greeted cautiously. "Your Majesty."

Kaeto lifted his chin in acknowledgement, but he didn't move otherwise.

"What time is it?" I rasped, blinking at the bright light streaming in from outside.

"Midday," Orlene said, still eyeing Kaeto warily.

"How's Val doing?" I asked, dragging my wits together—whatever was left of them at this point, anyway.

"He was awake when I looked in on him, but feeling about as terrible as you might expect. He fell asleep after a few minutes—but he seemed lucid, and he was able to eat and drink a bit."

It was about as good a report as I could have hoped for, under the circumstances.

"That sounds promising," I said. "I suppose we need to start discussing our next steps, now that we're here." I scrubbed at my face, willing myself to wake up properly.

"Right now, our next steps consist of cleaning up and making you presentable enough to be taken seriously at a high-level strategy meeting," Kaeto said.

"I wouldn't say no to getting rid of the stench of river sewage," Orlene replied. "But we're not leaving the dragons here unattended."

"One might almost think you still didn't trust me." Kaeto arched a brow. "I will have the servants bring a bathtub and hot water here for you, in that case. Firebrand—I trust you will accompany me while your comrade watches over the beasts?"

"Why not?" I said. "If nothing else, I imagine Aelio would like a word or twenty with me."

"No doubt," Kaeto agreed.

"A tub and water wouldn't go amiss," Orlene said. "Don't worry about heating it, though. We've got a more efficient way." She tipped her chin sideways, indicating the dragons resting behind her.

"A novel use for dragonfire, but no doubt the servants will appreciate the reduction in their workload." Kaeto rose and gazed down at me. "Shall we, then?"

"You're good here?" I asked Orlene, as I reached for my boots.

She nodded. "I'll keep an eye on things. See you in a few hours. Don't do anything I wouldn't do."

That last part was delivered in such a flat tone that it could only mean she already suspected me of having done something foolish. In her defense, she was probably right about that.

Still, there was something to be said for getting closer to the man who remained our best bet of finding and retrieving the stolen dragon eggs. Also, it looked like I might get a hot bath and some fresh clothes out of the deal, so there was that.

I finished lacing up my stolen boots and threw Orlene a jaunty salute. It seemed a safer response than pointing out that when it came to the question of engaging in inappropriate sex with me, she didn't have a lot of moral high ground to stand on.

Neither did Valeph.

Neither did a lot of people, if I was being honest.

After a quick check on the dragons, I fell in next to Kaeto, looking around at the garrison compound with interest.

I wondered what sort of troop numbers were housed here.

"There is no palace in the city," Kaeto said. "The port magistrate has offered the use of his dwelling, but I prefer to stay here in the garrison under the circumstances."

"Probably wise," I told him. "How's the city faring after the siege?"

"Not as badly as it might have done." Kaeto indicated a building to our right, and I followed him toward the entrance. "My brother's forces only arrived a few days ago. There wasn't time for the supplies of food or fuel to be exhausted."

"I guess it's good we arrived when we did, in that case," I said.

Servants bowed low and swept open the double doors of the structure, revealing a decently sized bath house within. At the feeling of steamy humidity against my skin, I wanted to groan in relief. Orlene wasn't the only one in a hurry to wash away the stench of the river.

"Bring practical clothing suitable for this dragonrider and leave it in the changing room. Other than that, we are not to be disturbed," Kaeto told the attendants, who murmured their assent and closed the doors behind us.

I went through to the changing room in question and started shedding clothes, not particularly caring if one of the servants came back to drop off fresh clothing and got an eyeful in the process.

"Gods," I said. "I don't think I've ever felt so filthy after being immersed in water."

I turned to find Kaeto watching me with that intent expression he sometimes held.

"I really hope you're not expecting me to attend you in the bath like I did that first night," I said dryly.

He snorted. "We have rather come full circle, have we not?"

But he only tossed me a towel to wrap around myself, before removing his own simple clothing and winding a towel of his own around his waist.

Rhyth, the city where I'd grown up, had a bathing culture not dissimilar to Alyrios. The garrison's bathing house wasn't fancy, but it had the familiar layout of a sluice area supplied with soap to rinse away dirt and sweat, followed by a steam room, a cold plunge pool, and sunken hot baths.

I set my towel aside and scrubbed the weeks of travel grime from my hair and skin, letting the stream of lukewarm water trickling from overhead wash everything down the drain. Forgoing the sauna and the cold plunge, I headed straight for the hot baths and lowered myself into the sunken pool with a happy sigh.

Like Kaeto, I was a mass of bruises and strains from the past few days. Steaming water closed around me in a comforting embrace as I settled onto the submerged bench ringing the outside of the tile-lined pool.

Bliss.

The sound of light splashing a few minutes later announced Kaeto's arrival. I peeled my eyelids open as he lowered himself onto the bench opposite me.

"How's the back?" I asked, not willing to pretend I hadn't scratched the shit out of it while riding his cock a few hours ago.

He grunted. "Better than the knee. And the jaw. And the ribs."

"Fair," I said.

While I hadn't made any attempt to resist his advances, the entire interlude still struck me as a bit bizarre.

"You really thought I was lying to you about Aelio all this time?" I asked.

He let his head fall back to rest against the lip of the pool. "I couldn't afford to believe otherwise. I told you—I've spent a lifetime being lied to by the people around me. Either they were trying to control me, or they were trying to manipulate me by telling me whatever they thought I wanted to hear."

"You were quick enough to believe me when I told you that someone was plotting to take your throne," I pointed out, bewildered. "I got that information directly from Aelio, you know—right before I sent him and his surviving soldiers here."

Kaeto lifted his head to look at me. "You could have tortured that information out of a captured raider. One look at that beast of yours and any prisoner with half a brain would start spilling secrets like water from a cracked pitcher."

I pondered that for a moment, frowning.

He waved a languid hand. "It made sense that the attack in the ravine was part of a larger plot. The raiders' forces were far too numerous and well organized."

I thought of a princep growing up surrounded by lies and conspiracies. "You've never trusted anyone in your life, have you?"

A short, bitter sound that might have been a laugh emerged from Kaeto's throat, half-stifled. "Not since I was too young and naïve to know better."

"Not even Aelio?" I asked.

He hesitated. "Aelio served my older brother before I assassinated him. He would have cut me down to save Proclus' life, had he been in a position to do so."

"He was the palace tribuni," I said. "Protecting the rightful emperor was his *job*."

"Yes," Kaeto allowed. "It's true that he's given me no reason to doubt his loyalty since he swore allegiance to me. Or at least, none that I know of."

It struck me suddenly as being unutterably sad that this man—this ruler—didn't even feel that he could trust the person who seemed to be his closest advisor and confidante.

"Aelio doesn't really strike me as the conniving sort," I said gently.

Kaeto's smile was a twisted thing. "The best connivers never do." He took a deep breath, as though to center himself. "However, as I said, I have no reason to doubt his trustworthiness, and many reasons to be thankful that you saved him. I misjudged you in that regard."

And when he'd realized I hadn't been lying about rescuing Aelio and his men, he'd apparently been so grateful that he felt the need to ravish me against a post—travel grime, river-water stench and all. There were undercurrents here that I hadn't grasped yet, and I had an unpleasant suspicion they had to do with the kind of emotions I was ill-equipped to understand.

I was going to have to pick this situation apart with Val's help, once he was sufficiently recovered—and that wasn't a conversation I was particularly looking forward to having. In the meantime, though, there was the small matter of Kaeto being a fugitive with a massive target painted on his back.

"Have you talked to Aelio about what to do next?" I asked. "Strategically, I mean."

"Yes," Kaeto replied. "However, the answer to that question does depend rather heavily on whether you're ready to ally your forces to mine and fly your dragons to Amarius, so we can burn Bruccias and his traitorous hangers-on to ashes."

THIRTY-ONE

"**Y**eah, no," I said. "Sorry, but that won't be happening. Roasting an unsuspecting mercenary army surrounding a far-flung river port is one thing. Flying headfirst into a well defended city with a massive contingent of dragon harpoons is another. Especially since Bruccias will find out what happened here within days."

This wasn't an exchange I particularly wanted to have while sitting naked in a bath. However, it was important that Kaeto not get his hopes up regarding his own convenient dragon army. Three dragons could cause a fair amount of devastation, as we'd recently proved. But they weren't invincible.

Kaeto's face had gone still, almost statue like. But after a short pause, he nodded as though it was the answer he'd expected—if not necessarily the one he'd wanted to hear.

"It's true that any element of surprise we might have possessed is well and truly spoiled at this point," he said. "How odd to think of my father's dragon harpoons finally seeing use after all these years. Bruccias and I used to sneak up to the ramparts to gawp at them when we were boys."

I suppressed a shudder. "I assume they've been well maintained since then."

"My father ordered them thoroughly overhauled and serviced when Utrea broke the treaty by once more breeding dragons," Kaeto replied. "I've kept them in readiness since my rise to power. Alyrios is beset by the beasts on two sides, after all."

I was well aware of that. Xael had been part of the first clutch of hatchlings brought to Eburos by my aunt and her concubines. With Frella's marriage to the king of Utrea, our two nations had become close allies when it came to all things dragon related.

"Three dragons won't be enough to take Amarius," I said firmly. "The only way to break that kind of harpoon defense is through force of numbers… which we don't have. And if we did, I'd still say no, because the losses would be devastating."

"An effective deterrent, then." Kaeto sounded sour.

"Eburos and Utrea raised dragon armies to keep Alyrios from invading *their* territories," I told him. "Not because they plan on invading *yours*."

He let his head fall back on the edge of the hot pool again. "I'm well aware. I thought we had achieved a rather stable equilibrium, these past few years. I simply cannot fathom why either of my idiot brothers seemed so hell-bent on throwing things into disarray."

I raised an eyebrow, not that he was looking at me. "Hereditary insanity?" I suggested.

He made a wordless noise somewhere between irritation and agreement.

"Mind you," he said, "I might have been less sanguine had I known that a group was secretly acquiring their own dragons, outside of the jurisdiction of regional governments."

"Two groups, if we count Bruccias and his stolen eggs," I shot back, aware that my lie about my comrades and I being free agents might yet come back to haunt us.

Kaeto grunted. "As you say." He roused himself abruptly, pushing his body out of the water with lean, sinewy arms. "No doubt your clothing is ready. We should return to the main garrison and continue this discussion with Aelio's input."

I prepared myself to leave the comfortable warmth of the bath and return to practicalities. "Yes, all right. I should go check on Valeph first, though."

☙ ♛ ❧

I dressed, mildly surprised when Kaeto accompanied me to the healer's rooms. There, we found Valeph—somewhat unexpectedly—deep in conversation with Aelio… albeit a rather one-sided conversation since Val could only manage a few words at a time before he started coughing.

"Sire," Aelio greeted, rising from his chair and bowing from the waist. "Darra. Hello. I see the quartermaster was able to find you something more appropriate to wear than servants' attire."

"Or stolen raider's clothing," I agreed. I'd been a bit worried that the attendant would bring me something completely ridiculous like a dress, but apparently 'practical clothing' for a dragonrider leaned more toward scout's leathers. That suited me just fine. "We didn't expect to find you here," I went on. "How's the leg doing?"

Aelio's expression turned rueful. "As well as could be expected, I suppose. I could probably ride a horse at this point, assuming I had someone available to help me mount. Nevertheless, the physic requires me to come in every couple of days so he can poke and prod at it."

"Be happy it's your leg and not your lungs," Val wheezed. "Your Majesty. I'm afraid any attempts on my part to either rise or bow would only result in low comedy." He paused, his body shaking as he tried to suppress a wet cough.

"I'll let it pass, just this once." Kaeto's tone was dry, but not particularly sharp.

"I wasn't able... to thank you properly before for saving me," Val managed hoarsely.

Kaeto waved a dismissive hand. "We'll consider the score even, after your actions during the fight at the gate of the imperial quarter," he said. "Let us speak no more about it."

"What does the healer—" I caught myself. "I mean, the *physic*—say about your lungs, Val? Is the medicine working?"

Approaching footsteps preceded a voice filtering to us from the interior doorway. "The physic says he needs to stop overexerting himself by talking too much." The man in question entered, taking in the small crowd gathered in his treatment room. He turned his glower on Aelio. "He also says that *you* need to avoid climbing steep stairways and standing on ramparts during a dragon attack."

Aelio raised an eyebrow, a glint of humor in his tired eyes. "And *outside* of dragon attacks?"

The physic appeared unamused. "That depends entirely on how invested you are in not walking with a permanent limp, young man."

"Message received," Aelio told him. "In my defense, the circumstances were rather extraordinary."

"Hmph." The man lifted a small clay pot with a cork stopper. "Here is the new salve. Apply it morning and evening. Now, if you would all remove yourself from this sickroom, my patient needs rest."

I glanced at Kaeto from the corner of my eye, abruptly aware that the physic must not have heard the first part of the conversation. He had no idea who Kaeto was, and I wondered what the emperor would choose to do about that. The answer, apparently, was nothing.

Aelio drew breath as though to inform the man of his visitor's identity, but Kaeto cut him off before he could.

"Quite right," he said. "Aelio, we must discuss matters, but perhaps not here."

"I'd like Orlene to be in on this, too," I said. "Val—concentrate on getting better. I'll fill you in on the details later."

"I trust so," Val rasped, his expression growing tart.

I still needed to pick his brain about Kaeto's strange behavior, as well—but that unbearably awkward discussion would have to wait.

"Sleep well, my friend," I told him and followed the others out.

We slowed our pace to match Aelio's. He was carrying the walking staff he'd been leaning on when I'd first seen him descending from the city's defensive wall, but he wasn't making use of it. His injured leg seemed capable of bearing weight well enough, but his limp was still pronounced. By contrast, Kaeto's limp was barely noticeable after whatever rest and treatment he'd received since our arrival.

Aelio's incisive eyes cut to me. "Tell me, Darra—does your organization have many former Eburosi priests as members?"

So, Kaeto must have given the tribuni quite a comprehensive report of recent events, then.

"Not many, no," I said.

He nodded. "And how is old Caius doing these days?

I hid an internal wince. A comprehensive report, indeed.

"I've not seen him in some time," I said airily. "Last I heard, he was living in the country, breeding fine horses and hunting dogs."

Aelio made a faint, choked noise. The sound that came from Kaeto's direction was more like a growl.

"Hunting dogs, you say?" Aelio's voice was deadpan.

I shrugged. "That's what I heard." I didn't mention the part where he came to the city several times per week to train new Eburosi recruits in military skills and strategy.

"How very idyllic," Kaeto said, in a tone that could strip paint. "I wonder what he would think if he could see his old home now?"

Probably that you should have killed Bruccias when you had the chance, just like you've killed everyone else who was in your way, I thought.

Aloud, I said, "I imagine he'd be glad that it's someone else's problem and not his."

"On which note," Aelio put in, neatly deflecting the subject to something more practical and less fraught, "I assume the emperor has already put his proposal to you."

"I did, and she refused," Kaeto said flatly.

"Ah." Aelio's handsome features hardened. "Well, that certainly makes things a bit more complicated, doesn't it?"

THIRTY-TWO

The impromptu council of war took place under a canopy that had been hastily erected on the parade ground. This allowed Orlene and me to keep an eye on the dragons. It also allowed Kaeto to impress upon the port magistrate just how much power was at his disposal, even though he'd been deposed by his brother.

Aelio had laid maps across the table that had been brought in for that use. In addition to the magistrate and his secretary, two senior members of Heleva's city council were also present. Kaeto, Orlene, and I rounded out the contingent.

"In the absence of an effective force to take the fight to Amarius," Aelio said, "we are essentially faced with forming a government-in-exile. Emperor Kaeto remains the rightful ruler of Alyrios and its territories. His brother Bruccias is attempting to hold power by claiming Kaeto was killed by raiders while en route to Heleva."

The port magistrate and the two council members looked alarmed.

"And you wish to form that government-in-exile... *here*, Your Majesty?" the magistrate asked.

"That has yet to be determined," Kaeto said. "Recent events have proven that the troops normally housed in the city's garrison aren't sufficient to repel a larger siege force."

"We didn't have dragons then," Aelio replied, his gaze landing heavily on me and staying there.

I returned it impassively, aware that my decision to use our dragons to break the siege on the city meant it would be nearly impossible to protest that we were impartial going forward.

The female council member—Bastina of the weavers' guild, as she'd been introduced—wrung her hands together nervously. "Your Imperial Majesty… we are grateful for the dragons' intervention. But large swathes of our crop and timberlands have been burned. Some are *still* burning."

Her fellow council member, a dark-haired man with a scar running down his cheek from a missing eye, nodded in agreement. "My colleague is correct. While I don't doubt that the dragons could defend the city from future attacks, every battle injures Heleva at the same time it injures the enemy."

The magistrate looked uneasily between his council members and his emperor. "We are still a port city," he said. "Trade accounts for the bulk of our economy. Food and timber can be shipped in if necessary."

Orlene grunted. "Sure, they can. Unless Bruccias places a blockade twenty miles upriver and twenty miles downriver to cut you off."

"Exactly," Aelio agreed, with a nod of respect to Orlene.

The magistrate looked ill. "Would he do that?"

"Of course he would," Kaeto said sharply. "I also wouldn't put it past him to ship dragon harpoons down here by barge in preparation for his next attack."

Aelio's hard gaze returned to me. "How certain are we that Bruccias knows the emperor Kaeto is here in the city?"

That was a good question.

"He knows Kaeto is alive," I said slowly. "He would have received a report after we attempted to breach the imperial quarter in Amarius, and successfully got away afterward."

"That's a long way from knowing that His Majesty is in Heleva," Aelio pointed out.

"True," I agreed. "It may not be a huge stretch, though. It's possible he could have received word that I rescued Kaeto from the raider attack on dragonback. Xael and I destroyed the raider camp afterward, but they had plenty of time to get a courier out on horseback before we got there."

Aelio nodded, frowning. "And from there, it wouldn't take much of a logical leap to connect him to a dragon attack on the forces surrounding Heleva. I think, on that basis, we'll have to assume he is aware of our presence here."

"And that's assuming no spies based here in Heleva hopped on the first boat heading north to report everything to him," Orlene added dryly. "We haven't exactly been keeping his presence a secret since we arrived."

All three city officials blanched, glancing at each other with unhappy expressions.

The port magistrate cleared his throat. "Your Imperial Majesty... we are but humble servants of the empire. However, from the information shared here, I cannot guarantee Heleva's ability to stand against a sustained attack from your brother's forces."

He looked like he half-expected the pronouncement to earn him a quick trip to the executioner's block.

"No," Kaeto replied. "I don't suppose you can."

"We need to craft an alternate plan," Aelio said grimly. "The good news is, it will take time to get a report from here to Amarius, and more time for Bruccias to mount another large-scale attack."

Orlene shot me a significant look. I knew exactly what she was trying to convey, and also that I needed a discussion with her and Valeph before I made any promises to anyone.

I swallowed a sigh. "I have some thoughts, but I need to meet privately with my colleagues first."

Both Kaeto and Aelio gave me their full attention.

"That is, if you will permit it, *Your Majesty*," I added, unable to keep a hint of dryness from creeping into my tone.

Kaeto gave me a shrewd look. "I suppose it can be arranged, under the circumstances. We will reconvene here at the same time tomorrow."

"Great," I said, without much enthusiasm.

⤙ 👑 ⤚

The physic let us in to visit Val an hour after the evening meal, eyeing us with an expression that said we'd better not wear out his patient again. Val was awake, although the dark smudges under his eyes said he probably shouldn't be.

"We need to talk," I said in Eburosi, once the physic had retired from the room and closed the door. "I think we need to get Kaeto and Aelio across the border to Utrea."

Val's pale brows drew together. "Utrea? Not Eburos?" he rasped in the same language.

I cringed at the thought of putting Kaeto on the same island as Caius and Decian. "No. *Definitely* not Eburos."

"I think the first question to ask is whether you intend us to take Kaeto to Utrea in an official or an unofficial capacity," Orlene said.

She didn't look happy. But she also hadn't dismissed the idea out of hand.

I rubbed the bridge of my nose. "That… is actually a very good question. Arguments for and against telling him who we really are?"

"It depends quite a lot on whether you really think Kaeto's an ally now," Orlene said.

I nodded. "I haven't lost sight of the mission, if that's what you're asking. And, yes, I'm reasonably convinced at this point that Kaeto is our best chance of getting the stolen eggs back."

Val cleared his throat cautiously. "He does owe us," he rasped.

Orlene made a considering noise. "And just as he's our best chance to get what we want, we're also *his* best chance to get what *he* wants."

"Exactly," I agreed.

"Next question," Orlene said. "How likely is King Rathanii to lose his royal shit if we show up on his doorstep with the deposed emperor of Alyrios in tow?"

"Another excellent question." I sighed. "Let's just say, I expect he'd rather deal with Kaeto than Bruccias."

"Taking him to the king will make it hard to maintain the lie that we're not affiliated with Eburos or Utrea," Val said, and descended into coughing.

Orlene waited until he regained control of his lungs. "That's true. I think we'd have to tell him the truth at that point. And he may not be too happy about the fact that we misled him."

"You're right," I agreed. "But in our defense, it's not as though he didn't lie to us as well."

"True enough," Orlene muttered. "So, we're doing this?"

I turned to Val. "Objections?"

"Not... in principle," he wheezed.

"Then I guess we're doing this," I said. "Assuming Kaeto and Aelio agree, of course."

Orlene pushed away from the wall where she'd been leaning. "In that case, I want to get back to the dragons. Leaving them unattended here still makes me nervous."

I gave her a brisk nod. "Sounds good. I'll be along shortly."

Orlene dipped her chin. She gave Val a final glance before she left the physic's quarters, closing the door behind her.

When she was gone, Val turned a beady eye on me.

"Go on, then," he said, still speaking Eburosi. "Tell me what happened that you don't want Orlene to know about."

I took a deep breath and let it out, puffing my cheeks. "Right. So… I might've let the emperor of Alyrios fuck me last night."

Val screwed his eyes shut, and let his head fall back against the pillow with a soft thump.

THIRTY-THREE

"**S**ay that again, please," Val muttered, not lifting his head from the pillow or opening his eyes.

"You heard me the first time. Kaeto and I had sex last night," I told him. I'd known this conversation was going to be unpleasant for both of us. It only remained to see *how* unpleasant.

"Yes, I did," he agreed. "I was holding out hope that my fever had spiked, and I was hallucinating."

He started coughing again, so I helped him sit up, shoving the pillow behind his back. When the fit subsided, I sat on the edge of his cot.

"Don't talk. I'll try to explain," I said. "Or, rather, I'll tell you what happened, and when I'm done, *you* can try to explain. Because I don't have a single, solitary clue what's going on in that man's head."

I went on to outline how I'd been thrust into the position as Kaeto's body servant after neutralizing his would-be assassin at the imperial banquet. How he'd rebuffed me when I'd assumed the position would involve sexual availability as well as other forms of servitude. How he'd seemed intent on manipulating me into humiliating physical displays, while showing no arousal in response.

"Honestly, I assumed he only liked men," I told Val, frowning. "And after the whole *'kidnapping and repeated threats of horrific death via dragonfire'* thing, I figured he'd gone from being indifferent to actively hating me."

"You shock me," Val muttered.

"But… then I had to change my assumptions about his sexual preferences when the guards showed up to search Saleene and Zuri's brothel while we were hiding there," I went on. "He definitely responded to me when I climbed on top of him and pretended I was fucking him, but I got the impression he wasn't too happy about it. I didn't really give it much more thought until he showed up last night and enthusiastically ravished me against a wall." I hesitated. "Well, technically, against a post. Which I don't really recommend because of the danger of splinters, by the way."

Val waited for a moment to make sure I was finished.

"That does seem like a rather abrupt shift," he said.

"*Right?*" I agreed, nodding my head enthusiastically. "I asked him about it afterward. He said it was because I saved Aelio from the raiders."

Val's pale face crumpled into a confused frown. "He already *knew* you'd saved Aelio, did he not?"

I shrugged helplessly. "Apparently, he'd assumed I was lying about it to keep him compliant, and Aelio was actually dead. I guess a lot of people have lied to him over the years. Which is, you know, pretty sad and all… but I'm struggling to see why that would have any impact on whether or not he was interested in putting his cock in me."

Val crossed his arms, still looking thoughtful. A suppressed cough hitched his slender chest, but it didn't descend into a full-blown fit this time.

"Please don't take this the wrong way, Darra," he said. "But you're not the world's most astute observer regarding the connection between sex and emotions."

I sighed. "Yes, Val. That's why I'm here bothering you about it when you should be resting."

It was unfortunate that the best candidate to help me tease out these unseen undercurrents also happened to be a man who'd briefly fallen in love with me before realizing I had no idea what that even *meant*… and certainly no capacity to return his feelings in the way he wanted.

On the other hand, perhaps it was just as well that Val had also received training in the temple, long before we'd met. The Eburosi priest class acted as counsellors and educators when it came to sex and relationships. Traditionally, they were all eunuchs, as Val was—although that had begun to change over the last couple of generations.

Val's background had allowed him to recognize the issue in our one-sided relationship for what it was, thankfully before things had become too badly tangled. He'd thought we were exploring a romantic connection that might result in lifelong commitment. I'd thought we were friends who'd decided to start having sex because it was fun.

Many deep and uncomfortable discussions later, I still couldn't wrap my head around the idea of there being different kinds of love. Whatever kind supposedly resulted in stomach butterflies and heartfelt romantic pining simply... didn't exist for me.

I liked sex. If someone wanted to have it with me and they were reasonably attractive, I was generally all for it. I'd learned the hard way over the years that if the person who wanted sex with me was also a friend, it usually meant there were going to be painful complications afterward, when I couldn't provide the other nebulous things that they expected of me.

"All right." Val regarded me with bloodshot eyes, and less open judgment in his expression than I might have feared. "Believe it or not, I did do a fair bit of research into this subject, after you and I untangled our... *misunderstanding*."

I winced.

"In addition to people who don't experience an association between sex and romantic connection, there are also those who embody the other side of that coin," he said.

"How do you mean?" I asked, trying to puzzle out what that would even look like.

"Some of the priests I spoke with described individuals who don't experience sexual attraction toward anyone," he went on. "Many eunuchs, for instance... though not all, as you're already aware."

He was talking about himself, but I'd known of others in the Priests' Guild who were perfectly happy to lie with men, women, or both. I nodded, still not clear where he was going with this.

He took a cautious breath, rubbing at his sore chest. "But there are others who don't find anyone arousing… until they have first formed an emotional or romantic connection with the person."

A sinking feeling settled in my stomach. "You think Kaeto…?"

Val shrugged one shoulder. "I'm not in a position to read the man's mind, beyond telling you if he's lying or not when he's actually in my presence. But if his attraction hinges on first forging an emotional connection, and he has only recently realized that you are trustworthy when he previously believed you were not—it might fit."

Several reasons why this could become extremely complicated jostled for my attention.

"And now I'm about to tell him that I've been lying to him from the beginning about who we are," I said.

"Yes," Val agreed. "However, I'm not certain that directly turning down a powerful man's sexual advances would have ended particularly well, either."

He didn't insult me by asking if the encounter had been consensual. We both knew that if I hadn't wanted it, and Kaeto hadn't taken no for an answer, he'd have been nursing bruised testicles, at best… and severe burns from Xael's displeasure, at worst.

"This is going to be complicated as fuck, isn't it?" I asked, resigned.

"So to speak," Val deadpanned. He paused for a moment, then continued. "I almost hesitate to ask this—but how do you feel about him? As a person, that is; not as part of a mission."

He just *had* to bring *feelings* into it, didn't he? My expression screwed up as I tried to unravel my opinions about Kaeto.

"He's an arsehole," I began. "He's also decent in a fight, and braver than I assumed he'd be." And then, because I couldn't *not* take this into account, "He saved your life when he didn't have to."

Val watched me in the way that always made it seem like he knew more about me than I knew about myself.

"That's all true," he said—and from him, the confirmation of verisimilitude held more weight than it did from most other people. "I'm fairly certain I saw Kaeto save *your* life, too."

He had, damn him. During the fight at the gate to the imperial quarter, Kaeto had blocked a blow that would have taken my head off.

"Yes. He did," I admitted. "He's still an arsehole, though."

An arsehole who was darkly attractive and surprisingly good with his prick.

"It sounds like I don't have to tell you how knotty this situation could become," Val said.

"No, you don't," I told him.

He nodded. "That said, he's an emperor—assuming he gets his throne back, anyway. I suppose that limits the likelihood that he'll try to pursue anything serious with you while he still thinks you're a commoner."

"I *am* a commoner," I said.

"You're the daughter of the three *de facto* heads of the Council of Rhyth," Val replied patiently.

"One of whom is a shapeshifter," I retorted. "Even if my family's political influence was enough to interest him, I sincerely doubt Kaeto of all people would be interested in mixing with pagan shapeshifter bloodlines."

"You're probably right," Val allowed. "Just… please try not to lead him on?"

That stung, even though it shouldn't have.

"It's not as though I threw myself at him." I couldn't keep the note of defensiveness out of my tone.

"No, of course not," Val said, placating. "Let's just focus on getting him out of danger. Once he's safely in Utrea, this whole thing will become a problem for the diplomats, not us."

"Please, gods, let it be so," I replied, the words heartfelt.

THIRTY-FOUR

Orlene and I both slept in the storage room near the dragons that night, taking turns keeping what was probably an unnecessary night watch. Whether Orlene's presence acted as some sort of subtle imperial deterrent, or whether Kaeto stayed away for other reasons, I wasn't sure.

Whatever the case, the first hint of a gray dawn saw us awake and preparing for the day.

Are we leaving soon? The question was a friendly nudge against my thoughts. The dragons had been content to lounge around the garrison's parade ground, eating the occasional pig or goat that was thrown their way and soaking up the awe of random onlookers. But Xael could feel my restlessness, nonetheless.

I think so, I told him.

With passengers? Xael pressed.

Probably. If Kaeto agreed to flee to Utrea, I guessed we'd be taking Aelio as well. Half-healed knee or no, I doubted the palace tribuni would let himself be separated from his imperial charge again anytime soon. *We'll go visit Aunt Frella. Who knows, maybe you'll find a pretty female dragon there to mate.*

That sally was met with an air of supreme indifference. I didn't push the issue. It wouldn't have made a difference.

Xael's lack of interest in breeding was something of a sore point, given how few dragons were left after Rathanii's grandfather had slaughtered his entire dragon army and put out a bounty on the eggs.

My little team was made up of misfit dragons.

There was Xael, who wouldn't mate at all. Also, Panosh, who'd been gelded shortly after hatching so he wouldn't pass on whatever condition had resulted in his missing front leg. And finally, Rensa—who only had eyes for Panosh, and had a history of attacking any other male dragon that tried to court her.

Foolish optimist that I was, I'd half hoped Rensa would eventually warm to Xael solely due to proximity, and vice versa.

No thank you. I like my male parts firmly attached, came the response. *Not to mention, unbitten.*

I couldn't really argue with that, so I left it alone.

Orlene asked me for directions to the bath house and headed out to have a proper wash. I accepted the simple breakfast delivered by a nervous, stammering soldier, propping myself against Xael's scaly haunch while I ate and pondered the logistics of what we were planning.

In the end, I could only devote so much energy to worrying about diplomatic incidents and the breakdown of the continent's fragile peace before I needed a distraction. Normally, I'd go flying… but drawing attention to dragons in the sky over Heleva didn't seem like the best plan, under the circumstances.

When Orlene got back from her soak, I handed over her half of breakfast and went for my own bath. That only ate up an hour or so of time, leaving a few more hours until our afternoon meeting with Kaeto and the port magistrate.

"How about a sparring session?" I asked Orlene, since I at least felt like a functioning human being today, after a couple of solid days of food and rest.

Plus the sex, of course—but I wasn't thinking about that part.

Orlene grunted agreement and went to grab a couple of practice swords. The two of us staked out a corner of the parade ground and fell into the rhythm of training, the clack of wood-on-wood reassuring in its familiarity.

Orlene was about half again my size, and mostly made up of pure muscle. She could snap me in two if she wanted, and she put me to shame when it came to fighting with either hand-and-a-half or two-handed swords. That made her an excellent sparring partner, since I couldn't afford to let my guard down or allow my concentration to slip.

We passed a pleasant stretch of time that way, sweating despite the day's cool cloudiness. The ache in my muscles reminded me that even with the respite since we'd arrived in Heleva, my body had been abused pretty thoroughly in recent weeks—and not just in the fun way.

"Is this sparring session open to anyone?" Kaeto's dry voice interrupted my thoughts, and I stepped back, disengaging.

Orlene grunted. "Pretty sure sparring with royalty is above my pay grade."

"I'm game," I said… probably unwisely.

"I'll give you a match whenever my damned leg improves enough to stand it," Aelio told Orlene. "I'm not familiar with that style of two-handed grip."

She let out a snort. "People on the continent call it the barbarian grip. And you're on. I do *love* disarming pretty boys."

Aelio would have been within his rights to show offense, but instead he only laughed. "Ha! Now you're just flattering me. For the record, I don't think I was ever the former… and I haven't been the latter in a very long time."

With both Kaeto and Aelio here, we had no reason to hold back on sharing our proposal regarding escape to Utrea. "Orlene? Do you want to fill Aelio in on our plan, while I talk to His Imperial Majesty?"

"Which parts of our plan?" Orlene asked cautiously.

"All of it," I told her, since there was really no more point in dissembling.

"If you say so," she said, handing me her practice sword. "Are there any maps around here we can use?"

Aelio glanced at Kaeto, who nodded permission.

"There should be a full set in the garrison commander's rooms," Aelio said. His gaze slid to me, landing heavily. "Please try not to actually maim each other?"

I wrinkled my nose at him. "I've expended too much energy keeping him alive to poke holes in him now."

"If I'm unable to hold my own against a slip of a barbarian girl in a sparring session, you've only yourself to blame," Kaeto added tartly.

Aelio still looked as though he half-expected calamity to strike the moment he turned his back, but he dutifully replied, "Of course, sire," and led Orlene toward the main barracks.

Alone with Kaeto, I flipped Orlene's carved wooden weapon and handed it over, hilt first. He accepted it, squaring off with me.

"Very well. What is this plan that you and your secretive friends have been hatching?" he asked.

Hatching, indeed. My expression soured at the unwanted reminder of our utter failure to complete the mission that had originally brought us here from Eburos.

"We want to fly you and Aelio to safety in Utrea," I said, feinting left to test Kaeto's defenses.

He parried easily, giving ground before offering a shallow lunge in response. I sidestepped, noting that he was still favoring his left knee slightly.

For a long moment, he didn't answer — focusing instead on feeling out my range. We traded another lackadaisical series of blows, falling into sync with each other's speed and force.

"My instinct is to resist," he said at last. "Leaving Alyrios feels too much like accepting my brother's victory." The wooden swords clacked, our sallies gaining strength as we got each other's measure.

"But?" I prompted, ducking and spinning to redirect a strike.

Another pause. "But… staying here will only ensure heavy damage to an important port city."

I saw an opening and lunged, Kaeto's wooden blade turning mine away at the last moment.

"There is another issue, though," he said. "I'm not certain that being a fugitive in Utrea is an improvement over being a fugitive in Alyrios."

I gave ground, steeling myself for the next admission. "Yes. About that."

Kaeto made a wordless noise that somehow exuded cynicism. "Yes," he echoed. "*About* that. You have given me the truth about something that matters very much, Darra Firebrand. However…"

He darted forward, fast as a snake. Our wooden swords slid together, catching on the rough crossguards. Then his free hand caught my wrist, holding with an iron grip. A gasp slipped past my control as he stared at me with sharp gray eyes — our faces mere inches apart. "… perhaps you would care to address the lies you have given me regarding other matters."

My heart rabbited, beating far faster than the situation warranted. Instinct honed by years of training whispered countermoves in my ear — *knee to the groin, kick to the injured left knee, headbutt to the nose.*

Instead, I stayed still, allowing him to hold me trapped.

"Yes," I agreed. "While it's likely that they would disavow me if asked, I do, in fact, have connections to Utrea's ruling family. If we take you there under truce, King Rathanii will offer a diplomatic reception as long as you don't abuse his hospitality."

Kaeto stood perfectly still, his grip on me unwavering.

"Did Utrea send you to retrieve the dragon eggs?" he asked, his voice even.

"No," I replied. "They were aware of the mission, but Utrea is a neutral party in the matter. My ties to the royal family are by blood, not oath of loyalty."

"Eburos, then," he said, not phrasing it as a question.

I didn't reply, holding my expression bland and still.

His eyebrow quirked. After a moment, he released my wrist and stepped back. My skin tingled hot and cold at the sudden loss of contact—my body replaying memories that had nothing to do with sparring.

"You needn't confirm it," he said gruffly. He rested the sword point on the dusty ground, packed hard by the passage of many boots. "So. You will take me to Utrea, where I will be expected to throw myself on Rathanii's tender mercy and beg his assistance against my brother. In exchange for... what, exactly?"

"Not having to deal with a warmongering monster on the Alyrion throne?" I suggested lightly.

He considered that. "And would such a thing truly move the man? Our dealings since my own ascent to the throne have been, shall we say, *minimal.*"

"I really think it might," I said. "Seriously, do you believe *any* of your neighbors want Bruccias on the throne?"

There was another pause, before the tight line of Kaeto's shoulders loosened a modicum.

"No," he admitted. "I accept your assertion that Utrea and Eburos maintain their dragon armies solely as a defensive measure. It's not in anyone's best interest to have the so-called ruler of the empire rattling swords."

"Does that mean you'll let us get you out of here?" I asked.

He drew breath and held it for a beat. "Subject to consultation with my tribuni, yes. I will give you my final answer at the meeting this afternoon.

✙

The meeting consisted of the magistrate and the same two council members as the day before. Kaeto gave me a small nod of assent as Orlene and I walked in. From what Orlene told me, Aelio had been positively relieved by the proposal. It was fairly clear he'd convinced Kaeto in the interim.

The Helevan officials should be happy about it, anyway. The magistrate seemed stressed, as well he might be—and the woman from the weaver's guild looked positively haggard with worry.

I wanted to ask if she should maybe sit down, court etiquette or not. But Aelio was already rolling out maps on the table in the center of the pavilion, eager to get down to business.

"We have a new plan of action," he began, moving smooth, fist-sized stones to the corners to keep the maps from curling up. "First thing in the morning, Emperor Kaeto will—"

With no warning, Bastina of the weavers' guild reached up, drawing a thick, six-inch hairpin from her intricate iron-gray bun. Quick as a flash, she lunged, darting around the corner of the table with the makeshift weapon extended, its wicked point aiming directly at Kaeto's right eye.

THIRTY-FIVE

One of the stone paperweights was in my hand and flying through the air before my conscious thought caught up. It hit Bastina in the wrist, jerking her aim off course.

She managed to keep hold of her vicious hair adornment—but Kaeto got a hand up and grabbed her elbow, redirecting her bodyweight past him as he stepped smoothly sideways, avoiding her weapon.

After the first frozen moment of shock, both Aelio and Orlene had lunged for her as well. They grabbed her from either side. Aelio wrenched the hairpin out of her grasp and tossed it away, cursing under his breath as her struggles threw his weight onto his bad leg.

"Your Imperial Majesty!" Heleva's magistrate sounded appalled. "Are you injured?"

Kaeto looked like he wanted to murder someone, but he straightened and brushed imaginary dust from his tunic as Bastina was wrestled to her knees on the packed dirt floor.

"No," he said, then snapped, "Don't touch that, you fool!"

The magistrate, who'd been reaching for the hairpin Aelio had tossed on the table, jerked his hand back as though it had been burned.

"It's probably poisoned," I explained, and the man's face went abruptly pale.

Kaeto's angry eyes flicked to me. "Well, Darra Firebrand," he said. "I do believe this is where we came in."

I blew out a rueful breath. I'd first come to Kaeto's attention when I'd foiled an assassination attempt in his own palace. It appeared that we had, indeed, returned to our beginnings.

"So it is," I agreed. "Next question—was this attack personal, or did someone else put her up to it?"

Bastina had collapsed in on herself, sobbing… her body hanging limp in the others' grip.

"I've no idea," Kaeto said. "But I do *so* look forward to finding out."

And right there, I heard the voice of the cruel ruler who'd once ordered his bastard half-brother torn apart by hunting dogs, and who'd sent a warship after two fleeing refugees to finish them off.

Apparently, I wasn't the only one to hear the threat behind the silky words.

"Your Majesty! I swear to you that I knew nothing of this!" The magistrate fell to one knee, bowing his head in abject supplication. The scar-faced council member was right behind him, although he didn't verbally grovel.

Kaeto made a noncommittal noise, which clearly did nothing to reassure the pair.

"Roll up the maps," Orlene said tightly. "The last thing we need is to give anyone here an outline of what we're planning to do."

I swept the other stones aside and did just that. "Have these two detained in the garrison," I said, jerking my chin toward the kneeling men. "Bring Bastina to where we're keeping the dragons. I'll get your answers for you, Kaeto."

Kaeto's hard eyes bored into me for a long moment before he gave a single, sharp shake of his head. "Do it," he told Aelio.

"I've got her," Orlene said, hauling the crying woman upright and twisting her arms behind her back. "Hard to drag a prisoner around while leaning on a walking stick, I imagine."

"That's the imperial palace tribuni you're talking to," I reminded her mildly.

"No, she's right." Aelio clenched his jaw and stepped away, rubbing at his knee. "Darra… you're on bodyguard duty. You certainly seem to have an aptitude for it." He turned to a group of soldiers running sword drills across the practice ground. "You there! Attend your emperor!"

The soldiers came jogging up, sweaty and wide-eyed.

"Take the magistrate and Councilman Rathgar into custody," Aelio snapped. "They are to be held until I personally order otherwise."

The soldiers glanced nervously at each other, then looked even more nervously at Kaeto.

"Yes, sir!" one of them said.

Within moments, the magistrate and the councilman had been chivvied away, leaving the three of us alone with Bastina. Silent sobs still wracked her chest, but she stood quiescent in Orlene's rough grip.

I wrapped the hairpin in a kerchief and pocketed it. Then I handed the rolled-up maps to Aelio, who stuffed them under his arm before taking up his walking stick.

"Let's go," I said grimly.

I nudged the link with Xael, who had been listening in with interest.

Need a human frightened? he asked. *Or fried?*

She's already frightened, I sent back. *But I need her terrified enough to tell us the truth.*

Xael gave a mental shrug of agreement.

We crossed to the corner of the practice field where the dragons were waiting. Without a word between us, Orlene flung Bastina onto the trampled grass. She cowered there, looking up in fear as the three great beasts ranged sinuously around her.

I stood at Xael's shoulder, with Kaeto and Aelio joining me warily. Orlene moved to stand next to Panosh, placing a hand on the male's scaly bronze neck. He snorted, blowing smoke, and Bastina cringed.

"Now," I said. "Tell us why you thought it would be a smart idea to poke the emperor of Alyrios with a hairpin in front of witnesses. Was it poisoned?"

Bastina clamped her lips shut, though her red-rimmed eyes were as wide as dinner plates as she stared up at the dragons.

When several seconds passed in tense silence, I said, "Xael?"

Xael puffed out his chest and shot a tiny spurt of flame at the ground. Bastina screamed as the hem of her ornate robes caught fire. She flailed around, beating at the flames with her bare hands until the fine cloth was reduced to smoldering ashes. I winced internally—that was going to be painful, especially for a weaver.

"Let's try this again," I said. "Was the hairpin poisoned?"

"Yes," she whimpered miserably. "I think so. He told me not to touch the point."

Now we were getting somewhere.

"*Who* told you not to touch the point?" Aelio demanded.

"I don't know," Bastina said.

I sighed. Xael drew in a great breath, his neck arching in clear threat.

"I don't know!" Bastina babbled frantically. "He didn't tell me his name! He said he was holding my brother hostage! He told me Branis would be killed if I didn't do this!"

Oh, blast.

"And you believed him?" Aelio asked, his tone emotionless.

Bastina bowed her head and nodded, cradling her burned hands loosely in her lap, palms up. "He showed me my brother's pendant. It was a gift from our parents when he achieved his guild certification."

Beside me, Kaeto made a low noise of irritation. "It appears my younger brother has learned some of my older brother's worst tricks. Assassination via dupe was one of Proclus' favorites."

"Kidnap someone's loved one and force them to do your dirty work for you," I muttered, disgusted. I turned back to Bastina. "Did the magistrate know about this? Or any of your fellow council members?"

She looked up at me blankly. "Of course not. If I'd told them, they would have tried to stop me."

"Well, *fuck*," I said, unable to hold it in.

"We did suspect there might be spies embedded in Heleva," Orlene said dryly. "Sounds like we were right."

It did indeed. Bruccias would have been an idiot not to sneak some of his own trusted agents into the city before blockading it. The news of our arrival must have spread like dragonfire throughout the city, leaving the perfect opening for one or more of the spies to act.

"I am satisfied that the attack did not involve anyone else in Heleva's government," Aelio said. "I suggest we remand the councilwoman into custody with orders to root out the spy network and, hopefully, retrieve her kinsman. Then, I think we should leave as quickly as possible."

Kaeto glared down his patrician nose at the woman on the ground, his expression conveying that he was balancing that suggestion with another one involving heads on pikes.

"Agreed," he said after a long moment.

❧ ⚜ ❧

In the end, it took the rest of the afternoon and evening to sort out the mess. Aelio set the garrison commander to finding Bastina's brother, assuming the poor sod was still alive.

If it hadn't been for Kaeto and Aelio, I would have suggested leaving for Utrea at night. However, I wasn't willing to risk inexperienced dragonriders in the dark, especially with one of them injured. We gathered our supplies for the journey in preparation for a predawn departure instead.

As the sky grew lighter in the east, the five of us gathered after a night of restless sleep. The situation was less than optimal, with two of us needing to ride double, Val still weak and shaky from his illness, and Rensa too small to carry two riders on a journey this long.

"Orlene, you're on Rensa," I ordered. "Val and Aelio, you're on Panosh. He can manage both of you for a few hours. *Your Imperial Majesty… you're with me.*"

At least I no longer had to worry about Kaeto knifing me in the back mid-flight.

Small victories. Xael's voice in my head held more amusement than the situation warranted.

You know, you're not nearly as funny as you think you are, I told him sourly.

Val eyed Aelio up and down. "You keep me from falling off, and—" A cough wracked him. "I'll keep *you* from falling off," he finished hoarsely.

"A fair bargain," Aelio replied, in solemn tones.

Val climbed onto Orlene's dragon, who helpfully fanned out a wing for him to use as a step up. Orlene helped Aelio clamber up behind him, her movements stiff with distaste in reaction to the physical contact with a man she barely knew.

"Is this all right?" Aelio asked uncertainly, wrapping an arm around Val's slender form.

"Don't be shy on my account," Val told him dryly.

Orlene patted Panosh's gleaming shoulder and went to mount up on Rensa. The small white dragon shook her head impatiently, eager to be off.

I double-checked that our supplies were firmly fastened over Xael's back before vaulting up and settling comfortably in place. Wordlessly, I extended a hand to Kaeto. He hesitated for only a moment before taking it and swinging up behind me. His arm settled around my waist, warm even through my borrowed scout's leathers. I tried not to think about the last time the two of us had been pressed close, heat against heat.

"It's past time to go. Let's fly," I said, turning Xael away from the rising sun and gripping with my knees.

With a piercing cry, Xael reared back and launched himself forward with powerful haunches, his massive wings catching the air as he flapped upward, leaving the ground behind us.

I looked left and saw Rensa's pale form rising eagerly into the sky, Orlene bent low over her graceful neck. I looked right and found Panosh soaring upward as well, seemingly unbothered by the two men clinging to his scaly back.

Beneath us, Alyrios grew smaller and more distant with every heavy, thumping wingbeat. Ahead of us lay Utrea, the hereditary land of the dragons... the home of my powerful aunt and her family.

"I do hope you know what you're doing, firebrand," Kaeto said, his hot breath tickling my ear as he spoke over the wind.

"So do I," I muttered, not sure if he'd be able to hear the words.

Around us, the sky lightened from pinkish gray to brilliant orange and blue as the sun breached the horizon at our backs.

finis

The story continues in *Mistress of War: Book 2*.

For more books by this author, visit
www.otherlove-publishing.com